Mark plopped on the couch. "So you'd met Grayson Sterling before?"

Just the sound of his name made her pulse flutter.

"At the shop a few weeks ago and then we sort of ran into each other at the park." Adrea chose her favorite paring knife and sliced a tomato. The sharp blade cut clean lines through the soft pulp. "He's had a standing order for his wife for six years."

Until a hit-and-run driver carved his heart apart, just like the tender fruit in her hands.

"He still buys the flowers even though she died?"

A knot formed in her throat. "He takes them to the cemetery."

"Sad." Mark looked at the floor.

"He always comes to sign the card personally." She arranged the slices on a saucer. "The salesclerks call him Prince Sterling, and his four annual appearances are the highlights of every year."

D0790481

SHANNON TAYLOR VANNATTER is a stay-at-home mom/pastor's wife/writer. When not writing, she runs circles in the care and feeding of her husband, Grant; their eight-year-old son; and their church congregation. Home is a central Arkansas zoo with two charcoal-gray cats, a chocolate lab, a dragonfish, and three dachshunds in weenie dog heaven. If given the chance to clean house or write, she'd rather write. Her goal is to hire Alice from *The Brady Bunch*.

Don't miss out on any of our super romances. Write to us at the following address for information on our newest releases and club information.

Heartsong Presents Readers' Service
PO Box 721
Uhrichsville, OH 44683

Or visit www.heartsongpresents.com

White
Roses

Shannon Taylor Vannatter

PROPERTY OF
G.T. CAMPBELL LIBRARY

Heartsong Presents

To my very own Pastor in Shining Armor for all your love and support.

I'd like to thank my mother, Veta Taylor; my critique partner, Lorna Seilstad; and longtime friends Ruby and Stephanie Garner for sharing their knowledge of flowers and florists.

A note from the Author:
I love to hear from my readers! You may correspond with me by writing:

Shannon Taylor Vannatter
Author Relations
PO Box 721
Uhrichsville, OH 44683

ISBN 978-1-60260-755-2

WHITE ROSES

Copyright © 2010 by Shannon Taylor Vannatter. All rights reserved. Except for use in any review, the reproduction or utilization of this work in whole or in part in any form by any electronic, mechanical, or other means, now known or hereafter invented, is forbidden without the permission of Heartsong Presents, an imprint of Barbour Publishing, Inc., PO Box 721, Uhrichsville, Ohio 44683.

All scripture quotations are taken from the King James Version of the Bible.

All of the characters and events in this book are fictitious. Any resemblance to actual persons, living or dead, or to actual events is purely coincidental.

Our mission is to publish and distribute inspirational products offering exceptional value and biblical encouragement to the masses.

PRINTED IN THE U.S.A.

one

"Whoa!" Adrea Welch teetered on top of the rickety three-step utility ladder. With both arms flung out, surfing style, she regained her balance and pressed a hand to her pounding heart.

"Let me hold that for you," a deep voice echoed from the back of the sanctuary.

The man hurried toward her. Emerald green eyes, windswept sable hair, and an irresistible cleft in his chin. Late-twenties, maybe thirty. Probably the groom. All the impossibly handsome men, especially the nice, mannerly ones who hung out in church, were taken.

Especially in tiny Romance, Arkansas.

But looks weren't everything and he might never have been in a church before, just here for the wedding. Underneath that heart-tilting smile, he might be a jerk.

"Thanks." She glanced down, making sure he wasn't helping as an excuse to check her out. He wasn't. Instead, he studied her work.

"I'm almost done." Adrea looped yellow roses through the white latticework archway.

"The church should invest in a better ladder."

"Actually, it's mine." She weaved ivy through the roses and climbed down. He was tall, at least six foot three. The top of her head came just about nose level on him.

"Are you in the wedding party?" He slung his jacket over one shoulder. Shirtsleeves, rolled up almost to the elbow, revealed muscled forearms.

"I'm the florist." Always the florist; never the bride. "Adrea Welch."

"A-dree-uh."

She nodded at the correct pronunciation. "Very good, but

I've been known to answer to Adrian and Andrea."

"It's nice to meet you, Adrea." He offered his hand. "I'm the pastor at Palisade over in Rose Bud. Grayson Sterling. Most folks call me Pastor Grayson."

She suppressed a gasp and shook his hand. Warmth spread over her at his firm, yet gentle grip.

"I'm sorry, have we met?"

"Um, I usually do the white roses."

The light in his eyes snuffed out.

Six years of standing orders for his wife's birthday, their son's birthday, and their anniversary. For the last two, he hand-delivered the flowers to the cemetery. And added Valentine's Day to mark the date of her death.

"Sara always treasured them and thought it so romantic to get flowers from Romance." His voice sounded forced. "Even though mine is always the same order, you make each one unique."

"I actually enjoy the challenge of making each array distinctive." *How lame. Might as well tell him I take pleasure in arranging flowers for his dead wife.* "She must have been a very special lady."

"Yes." He stuffed his hands into his pockets. "How long have you been at Floral Designs?"

"Seven years."

"I've been a patron and pastored the church almost that long." He frowned. "Odd that we've never met before."

"I hardly ever go out to the showroom, and only started decorating wedding sites in the last few months." She fluffed the swirl of tulle at the base of each brass candelabra to catch the rainbow of light reflecting through the lone stained-glass window.

"This is the first wedding I've agreed to officiate since Sara. . . So, you attend here at Mountain Grove?"

"From the time I can remember, and my sister's husband is the preacher." She cocked her head to the side, surveying the archway. Yellow roses were her favorite. Once upon a time, she'd planned to use them for her own special day.

She checked her watch. Almost time for the round of afternoon weddings to start. "I better get out of your way."

"Nice meeting you. I'll pick up Sara's arrangement later."

"It'll be ready." She hurried out of the church, slipping on her jacket. Preachers really shouldn't look so good. How could any self-respecting Christian female concentrate on the sermon? He definitely lived up to the romantic hero her employees mooned over every time he came to pick up the roses. No wonder the salesclerks called him Prince Sterling.

Adrea stashed empty boxes and transport forms in the back of the van.

Three down, three to go. And none of the nuptials were hers.

Her hometown thrived on weddings. Half her livelihood came from weddings. She was so sick of weddings.

A Valentine balloon bouquet tried to escape from the van. She punched a heart-shaped, pink foil number bobbing beside her head.

"Roses are red, my love," a tinny tune played. "Violets are blue-ooh. Sugar is sweet my love, but not as sweet as you."

She slammed the door shut.

Okay, time to count blessings. She started the engine.

Number one: She and her older sister had recently bought the floral shop. Number two: Since couples came year-round to get married in if-you-blinked-you-missed-it Romance, the town's notoriety made for a busy floral shop. Number three: It was Valentine's Day, their biggest day for weddings and roses.

Twenty-five and the co-owner of a successful business. Yet a sigh welled within her.

Just two years ago, she'd been the soon-to-be bride blissfully planning her own ceremony. Until three weeks before the big event, when Wade crushed her illusions with his curvy blond floozy, clad only in a towel.

She shook the thoughts away as she rounded the curve and turned into the lot at the post office. Adrea managed to get Mom's roses out of the van without any trouble from the balloons.

Samantha—just Sam—Welch stood at the counter with piles of wedding invitations threatening to topple.

"Hi, Mom." Adrea set a crystal vase on the counter.

"Hey, Baby." Mom's smile brightened and she stopped stamping long enough to inhale the fragrance of the dozen long-stemmed roses. "Your father."

"Is a very sweet man."

"Are you okay?" Mom's brow furrowed.

"I'm fine."

"Haylee thought you might need her to spend the night and said something about eating Yarnell's Death-By-Chocolate ice cream straight out of the carton."

Adrea's eyes misted at the thoughtfulness of her seven-year-old niece. "I'll have her over soon, but we won't need sinful treats. I'm fine. Really."

Mom chewed on the inside of her jaw and surveyed Adrea with her intense sapphire gaze. Unconvinced, she went back to hand-stamping the invitations with a practiced, speedy precision. The rhythm of *clunk, clunk, clunk* echoed through the small office, toiling out the results of Romance's other claim to fame. The remailing program.

Valentine's cards arrived in droves for the unique *Love Station* postmark only in use each February 1–15. Year-round, brides from all over the country mailed their invitations in overstuffed manila envelopes, just to have them remailed from Romance, Arkansas.

Mom had stamped Adrea's invitations and taken care of them when the plans deflated like a balloon detached from the air hose. She didn't know how Mom had handled it. Sent don't-come-to-my-wedding-it's-not-going-to-happen cards? Somehow, Mom had let everyone know the engagement was off and no one asked questions.

"I met the pastor at Palisade just now." Adrea grabbed a stack of finished invitations as they began a slow landslide and scooped them into two piles.

"That poor man. It doesn't seem possible two years have passed since his wife died."

Adrea nodded. "I heard he's thinking of resigning. Maybe Mark could apply for that church. Wouldn't that be perfect?"

"To us." Mom raised an eyebrow. "Your brother feels very strongly called to be an associate pastor."

"I'm so afraid he'll end up somewhere else." Adrea hugged herself. "I mean, he just came home, and there aren't any churches around here that have associates."

"Searcy has several." Mom's stamping never lost rhythm. "Don't worry, God will work it out and put Mark right where He wants him."

"You're right. I better scoot; it's our busiest day."

"Tell me about it." Mom stopped stamping long enough to massage her wrist.

❧

Adrea wiped away a tear, then turned to sweep the smattering of fallen leaves and trimmed stems from the workroom floor.

As always, the pale flowers made her grieve for a woman she'd never met. Especially since she'd met the man left behind. She buried her nose in the cool satin of a fragrant blossom then added a few more fern fronds to the plastic container.

From births to proms and graduations, running the floral shop thrust her into the middle of the lives of countless strangers. She delighted in her work. Except for Valentine's Day, funerals, and white rose days.

What must it feel like to be the object of such devotion? It was hard to fathom how a man could love a woman so much he placed a standing order to mark each special occasion then continued the tradition even after her death. She swiped at another tear.

Maybe she felt a kinship with Sara because she'd arranged the white roses for so long. *Or because Sara died on what should have been my wedding day.* She squeezed her eyes shut.

Their happily-ever-afters had vanished like vividly colored Valentine's balloons caught in a vicious wind and swallowed up by angry clouds.

She filled the holes between the roses with snapdragons and Queen Anne's lace. Turning the arrangement slowly around, she checked each side for balance.

The showroom door opened and her sister, Rachel, entered jostling two large balloon bouquets, looking as if she might float away like Mary Poppins. "These are for Mrs. Carlisle. Maybe I can get them delivered before she gets the chance to add something else to her order."

"Actually, she already called."

"Let me guess." Rachel tapped her chin with a forefinger. "She's invited four more people and needs us to whip up another centerpiece for her Valentine's dinner."

"*Six* more guests."

Rachel smoothed a hand over her hairdresser-enhanced auburn hair. "Guess I better get busy with the extra flowers."

"Already did it, before she ever called." Adrea picked up the fluted crystal vase filled with red roses and pink carnations from behind the counter and set it on the worktable.

The sisters high-fived.

Rachel tied a heart-shaped weight on both clusters of balloon ribbons. "Mom said you stopped by."

Adrea propped both hands on her hips. "Do y'all call each other as soon as I leave?"

"We're just worried about you. How many almost brides spend their time fulfilling the dreams of other brides?"

"I'm fine." *How many times have I said that today?*

Rachel handed her a tissue and picked up Mrs. Carlisle's centerpiece. "You're entirely too empathetic for this place."

Adrea glanced at the clock. The lavender butterfly on the second hand made slow progress visiting each silk blossom—surrounded number. Almost two o'clock. Anywhere else the gaudy business-warming gift from their brother would be too busy. Especially set against pastel wallpaper bursting with an astounding assortment of flowers. But for the workroom, perfect.

"Before you go, can you take the white roses out front?"

"Sorry, I'm fixing to make deliveries. Besides, the customers love it when the hermit comes out to visit." Rachel threaded the balloons through her fingers. "Can you give me a hand?"

Adrea helped load the van, then waved her sister off. Alone

in the back parking lot, the hair along the nape of her neck stood on end. Someone was watching. She scurried back inside and locked the door.

Just my imagination.

Silly. Rachel only had two nearby deliveries and would be back soon.

Adrea undid the bolt, and with jittery insides, picked up the white roses. She hated working with customers in the bustle of the showroom. It never failed, whenever she went out front, a client always cornered her with compliments. Nice, just not her style. She much preferred a thank-you card.

The back door flew open behind her. She spun around to see a man. His shaggy, dishwater blond hair hung almost to his shoulders in greasy clumps, hiding his eyes. She sucked in a breath to scream, but his hand clamped over her mouth.

"I didn't think I'd quite get that reaction." Wade's words slurred together.

If he hadn't spoken, she wouldn't have recognized him. Her gut twisted at a whiff of alcohol. She pushed his hand away, put some distance between them, and gulped deep breaths of blossom-perfumed air.

He'd lost weight. Gone was the handsome, well-groomed, charming man she'd once fallen in love with. Gone was the layered hairstyle, casually gelled back from his face. Gone was the self-confident golf instructor who'd put an engagement ring on her finger and promised to love only her. Wasted.

"What are you doing here? You're not driving like this?"

"I hitched a ride and waited until Rachel left, so we could talk."

"You were watching the shop?" She shivered. Someone spying on her, even someone she thought she knew, gave her the creeps.

"I knew she'd never let us talk in peace. Do you remember what day it is?"

How could I forget? Adrea closed her eyes, clutching the roses. "I'd like you to go now."

He steepled his hands, as if in prayer. "Please, Adrea. Our

second anniversary. Or it should have been anyway."

"Wade, just go. We're over. You're engaged to—someone else." She couldn't bring herself to say the name. "I have to take these roses out front."

"They can wait." He grabbed the white roses, and they crashed to the floor, flinging water and twisted flowers.

"Look what you've done!" Fresh tears stung her eyes.

"Hey, don't cry." He moved toward her, ready to provide comfort.

She sidestepped him.

He tried to pull her into his arms.

"Don't." She jerked away and slapped him so hard her fingers stung.

The connecting door to the showroom opened.

❧

Grayson hesitated, his gaze taking in the pretty florist he'd met at the church, the red handprint appearing on the man's cheek, and finally the ruins of a flower arrangement on the floor.

He shut the door behind him. "Excuse me, but we heard a noise—the clerks were busy so I offered to check. Is there a problem?"

"Who are you?" The man looked from Grayson to a jittery Adrea, suspicion clouding his eyes. He took a menacing step toward Grayson.

Drunk, disorderly, disheveled. The shop's back door stood open. Had this guy just wandered in off the street or did he know Adrea? Though Grayson barely knew her, she didn't seem like the type to hang out with drunks. Yet, the man seemed possessive toward her.

"Just a customer." Grayson offered his hand. "Grayson Sterling."

The man's jaw dropped. He stepped back. Without another word, he spun around and ran out the back door, slamming it behind him. Vase-laden shelves rattled in his wake, but nothing fell.

Odd reaction. Grayson turned back to Adrea.

With shaking hands, she pushed dark bangs out of her too shiny, midnight blue eyes.

"Are you all right?"

"Fine." Her voice quivered.

Anything but fine. "I realize it's none of my business, but should that guy be loose on the streets?"

"He's drunk, but he said he's not driving, and he'd never intentionally harm anyone." She stooped to retrieve the container from the heap in the floor. "I'm afraid I dropped your flowers."

He winced at the sight of the damaged roses, their heads forlornly nodding.

"I'm sorry. I'll make a new arrangement." A tear trickled down her cheek. She wiped it away. "It won't take a minute."

His gut twisted. "There's no rush. My son's begging to go to the park anyway." He knelt to retrieve errant leaves and petals. "Let me help you clean up this mess."

"That's not necessary." She grabbed several paper towels and sopped up the spill then took the refuse from him and threw it all in the trash. "I'll take care of it."

With trembling fingers, she plucked the flowers, ruined or not, from a block of foam and tossed them into a compost bin. She grabbed a contraption and began stripping the thorns from a few fresh roses on the counter.

He should go. But his feet wouldn't move. The handprint on the drunk's face proved she could take care of herself, yet she looked so shaken. So vulnerable.

She winced and blood dripped onto the translucent petals of a white rose.

"You're bleeding."

"It's nothing." Calmly, she removed the embedded thorn and popped the fleshy part of her right thumb into her mouth, only to gag. She crumpled the crimson-stained rose in her fingers and tossed it in the bin.

"Are you sure you're okay?"

"I'm fine. Really. And I'm sorry about the delay." She washed the puncture. With no paper towels left, she rubbed her palms down slender, jean-clad thighs and dug out a fresh roll from under the sink.

"It's not a problem."

The back door opened, and the clerk he usually saw in the showroom entered. She frowned when she saw him.

"Pastor Grayson? Is everything all right, Adrea?"

A blush crept up Adrea's neck. "I'll fill you in later."

"Good to see you, Rachel." He offered his hand. "I wondered where you were today."

"Just had a couple of deliveries."

"Well, I better get back to Dayne." What if the drunk came back? He ran his hand over his jaw and turned back to Adrea. "You really should consider locking the back door in the future."

Rachel's eyes widened.

"I'll come back in about forty-five minutes. No rush." With one more glance toward Adrea, he strolled back to the showroom.

❧

The door shut behind him, and Adrea darted to the floral refrigerator.

The perfect romantic hero. A knight in shining sterling.

But a deep sadness lurked in the emerald depths of his sparkling eyes. The knight had lost his lady.

Arms laden, she chose another container.

"What happened?" Rachel crossed her arms and leaned against the counter.

Adrea unloaded on the worktable and touched a tender blossom to her nose. "Nothing happened, other than some broken flowers."

"Okay, I'll bite." A storm brewed in Rachel's brown eyes. "How did the flowers get broken, and why did Pastor Grayson think you needed to lock the back door?"

"Wade stopped by," she squeaked.

Rachel propped her hands on slim hips. "Isn't he supposed to be in Missouri?"

"Probably just here to visit his mother." Though Helen

hadn't mentioned it. "He was drunk."

Adrea's gaze locked on her sister's.

The phone rang. Adrea reached for it, but the red light already glowed. One of the salesclerks had nabbed the call.

"I just don't want you falling for his 'poor me' routine." Rachel rolled her eyes. "I still can't believe you almost married him."

"Yes, but I didn't." She picked up the rose-stripper.

"Thank You, God." Rachel looked heavenward.

"Listen, I know you have this thing about trying to protect me, but I can take care of myself. I can handle Wade."

"You sure about that? You seem kind of shaky to me."

"I'd never seen him drunk before. He'd been sober for two years when we met." Adrea hugged herself. "He's like a different person." *And it's my fault he started drinking again.*

"The nerve of the jerk. Today of all days."

"Can we drop it?" Finished with the roses, she inspected her thumb. Another split nail, just from arranging flowers. Flimsy and paper-thin, they'd never recovered from her childhood nervous habit of biting. And Wade's visit made her want to do more than nibble.

"Are you sure you're okay?"

"It was just a thorn." Adrea held her hand out for her sister to see. "It's not even bleeding anymore."

"I didn't mean your thumb." Rachel touched her arm.

"I'm fine. Really." She took several cleansing breaths and slowly rotated the flowers to inspect them from every angle. Satisfied, she turned her back to the counter and leaned against it, begging her heart to slow. "Can you take the roses out front? And let's not charge him since he had to wait."

"Sure." Rachel picked up the arrangement and turned toward the showroom.

Adrea grabbed a heart-shaped crystal vase off the shelf. She filled it with red rosebuds, fern fronds, and baby's breath, then turned to the final bridal bouquet of the day.

She started with a cluster of fuchsia stargazer lilies in the center and worked them into a V shape. She loved the traditional cascading type rather than the popular rounded, hand-tied variety. It was what she'd planned to use for her wedding.

As the bouquet took shape, she imagined it in the trembling fingers of a blushing bride. She clasped it in front of her and stutter-stepped across the floor.

"Dun, dun, duh-duh. Dun, dun, duh-duh."

The showroom door opened and Adrea's measured stride faltered.

Helen's blue-tinged updo blended with her periwinkle suit. Southern Belle to the bone. She looked a good eight years younger than sixty-five.

With a wistful sigh, Adrea went back to the worktable to add more baby's breath. "I was just wondering why anyone would come halfway across the country to get married in Romance. We even have a couple coming from New York this year. Do they think the name of our town will guarantee their happily-ever-afters?"

"Someday"—Helen hugged her—"you'll make a lovely bride, with all that dark hair and creamy complexion. I'm sorry this is such a difficult day for you, dear. And I'm sorry about Wade. I told him to leave you alone."

"It was no big deal." She'd hoped Helen wouldn't learn of his visit to the shop.

"I so wanted you to be my daughter."

Adrea's chin trembled. "I so wanted to be your daughter."

Helen handed her several fuchsia ribbons. "Good news; I think Pastor Grayson has decided not to resign."

"Actually, I met him this morning."

"He's such a wonderful pastor." Helen clasped her hands together. "It's just been really hard for him since Sara died."

"Maybe God gave him a gentle nudge to stay in the ministry." Adrea threaded the satiny strands through the blossoms and snipped off the ends, leaving several trailing wisps shimmering along the stems. After final inspection, she wrapped the creation in white tissue paper and gently packed it in a large carton with the bridesmaids' bouquets.

She kneaded the tendons in her cramping hands and

turned to the numerous corsages and boutonnieres lining the worktable. With sore, raw fingers, she stuck long, pearl-studded pins into the stems of each one.

Helen tucked the finished product into clear cellophane bags.

Weddings. With vehemence, Adrea jabbed the pin into the groom's rosebud.

"Careful." Helen took the boutonniere from her. "You need a break."

"I do." Her stomach knotted at the irony of her words. "Two more weddings to deliver, then we're out of here."

❧

With Dayne tucked in bed, Grayson stood on the back porch, stroking Cocoa's velvety ears. The heavy dog leaned against his leg.

When he'd returned for the arrangement, everything seemed calm at the floral shop. The salesclerk had tried not to charge him, but he'd paid anyway.

Was Adrea okay? He couldn't get her trembling hands and voice off his mind.

He looked up at the stars and drained his coffee cup. Caffeine couldn't hurt him. He never slept anyway.

Stepping inside, he took off his coat and sniffed the air. Apple and cinnamon. Something baking, as usual, in the freshly painted pale peach kitchen. Sara's favorite color. But it wasn't the same.

He sat at the pedestal table and lay his face against the cool oak surface.

"Gray, you okay?" Grace's voice quivered.

"I miss the old house." He pushed up from the table. "I miss her."

Grace's slender arms came around his shoulders, and she rested her chin on top of his head.

His twin had given up her life to help with Dayne. She'd cut back her thriving catering business in Searcy and moved to Rose Bud with them. All for him. For his future. A future without Sara.

Only to hear him grumble about the new house because the air didn't smell of Sara's soft, sweet perfume.

"It's just a bad day." He ran his hands over the smooth wood. Sara had ordered the table from a catalog and waited three weeks for it to arrive. She'd made an adventure out of it by sewing a red and white checked blanket and serving picnics on the floor.

"I took her clothes to the Red Cross for hurricane victims this morning. But not the curtains she made. Even though they don't fit any of the windows here. . ." Grayson closed his eyes. "I just couldn't."

"I know it was hard, but you did good." She hugged him tighter. "Sara would be glad her things went to people who needed them."

He concentrated on not letting her feel the sobs welling within his chest.

Grace patted his shoulder. Grabbing his empty coffee cup, she walked over to the counter. "How was the wedding?"

"I pasted a smile on my face, joined the happy couple in holy matrimony, and took Dayne to the cemetery." Poor Dayne. A five-year-old shouldn't think it's normal to go to the cemetery on Valentine's Day.

He stared out the window at the inky sky. "I never imagined this day would be anything other than a joyous occasion for Sara and I to share a special, romantic dinner. Instead of celebrating with my wife, I left the church where we were married to place flowers at a cold, marble stone."

She poured a cup of coffee and added one teaspoon each of creamer and sugar. When she turned to face him again, her shiny eyes swam in unshed tears.

Lifelong friends with Sara, she hurt almost as bad as he did.

"I'm sorry. Maybe the move was a bad idea." She set the cup in front of him.

"It's not that." He took her hand. "I shouldn't have let the deacons talk me into staying at the church. I should have resigned back when Sara died."

"They don't expect miracles." She stepped behind him

again and massaged the tense muscles in his shoulders. "They know what you've been through."

"I need to seclude myself in the office and not come out until I have a sermon for Sunday. I need to go see Mrs. Jones, who recently lost her husband." *How can I comfort the grieving, when I still grieve?*

"Why don't you take them up on hiring an associate pastor?" Grace pulled a chair beside him and sat.

"Palisade has never had an associate."

"I know, but the church has grown, and I think it's high time you got some assistance."

An associate could hold the church together so I can fall apart in peace. Tempting. He could call his old professor for recommendations. See if there might be someone local. . .

"It's just the day. I'll be better tomorrow."

"We both will be." She kissed his cheek.

❧

The February morning air burned Adrea's lungs. Each breath formed a visible cloud as she jogged around the walking trail.

Another Valentine's Day behind her and she hadn't handled any weddings for two days. She silently thanked God for the much-needed reprieve.

With the park to herself, memories stirred of the many times she'd set up flowers for countless happy couples there. Maybe a jog wasn't such a good idea after all.

A cream-colored sedan pulled into the parking lot. A small boy in a marshmallow-puffed coat bounced from the car, followed by a chocolate Labrador retriever. A hooded man, probably his father, braved the frigid air. She looked away from yet another reminder of what she didn't have.

"No, Cocoa! Come back!" The boy's voice cut through the stillness.

"Dayne! Stop!" the man yelled.

As she turned toward the commotion, she saw the small boy, his little face awash in tears, chasing the Lab. Tongue lolling, the dog gained a huge lead, leash dancing behind.

Adrea gasped as the pair veered straight for the highway.

Darting from the path, she cut in front of the dog and stomped one foot solidly on the leash. She grabbed it before he could jerk it away and send her tumbling. Momentum threatened to propel her after the large animal, but she pulled with her entire body weight until he stopped.

The boy caught up, sniffling. As he buried his face in the dog's coat, the man joined them.

An incredibly handsome man. Grayson Sterling.

His breathing came in raspy wheezes. Young and in good shape, it didn't make sense for him to be so short of breath.

"Are you all right?"

He clutched his chest and opened his mouth. Only a gasp came out.

Why didn't I ever take CPR? She tried to remember what she'd heard about injuries he'd sustained in the wreck. Nothing to do with his lungs. Just his knee.

The boy stared wide-eyed, tears again coursing down his cheeks.

two

"Sit down here." Adrea motioned to a bench. Heart ricocheting, she grabbed her cell phone from her pocket. "I'll call an ambulance."

"No, don't." Grayson sucked in a ragged breath between each word. "I'm feeling better."

"You sure?"

"I tried to run and hurt my knee."

That didn't explain his shortness of breath.

His eyes darted to the little boy.

Taking his cue, she knelt to the child's level and tried to sound calmer than she felt. "He'll be just fine."

After several breaths, the gasping gradually eased. "With my bad knee, I can't keep up with these two. I could just see Cocoa running into traffic, with Dayne right on his tail."

Tires locked up and squealed nearby, as if for emphasis.

With a wince, he closed his eyes.

Adrea cringed, waiting for the crash. Thankfully, none came.

Grayson cleared his throat. "Dayne, did you say thank you?"

The boy turned his tear-streaked face toward her. "Thank you."

"No problem. I love dogs."

Several chocolate-colored hairs stuck to the boy's wet cheeks.

"Maybe you should take this." Adrea handed the leash to Grayson and fished a fresh tissue from her pocket to wipe away the fur and tears.

"We really appreciate your help." With his breathing returning to normal, he placed a firm hand on his son's shoulder. "Don't ever run off like that again, Dayne."

"Sorry, Daddy." The boy looked at the ground.

"If Cocoa ever gets away again, just call him. Once the squirrel climbed the tree, he would have come back if you had simply called him."

"But I don't want him to go to heaven, too." The boy's chin puckered.

A hard lump formed in Adrea's throat.

Grayson hugged his son. "He probably wouldn't have run into the street. He's smart. Full of life, but smart. From now on, I'll hold his leash."

"Okay."

Adrea watched in silence, until Grayson turned back to her.

"Sorry to drag you into our little melodrama." Grayson's voice fell flat. No life left. "Dayne, this is Adrea. She does Mommy's flowers."

The boy shook her hand. *Adorable.*

"At Miss Helen's store? She goes to our church."

"Actually, my sister and I just bought the shop, but Miss Helen still works a few days a week." She tweaked the child's cold-reddened nose. Though he was blond, he had his father's striking green eyes, paired with numerous dimples.

"Again, we appreciate your assistance today." Grayson clicked his tongue at Cocoa. "We better go; I need to get to the church and it's colder than I realized."

She watched him leave. *Going through the motions for his son's sake.*

&a.

Alone at the shop at the end of a long day, Adrea couldn't get her mind off the encounter with what was left of the Sterling family, though two days had passed. For six years, she'd created white rose arrangements for Sara and never met them. Now, she'd bumped into Grayson three times within a week. Weird.

She reached up to the top shelf to retrieve the silver-filigree keepsake box. Inside the red velvet lining, she dug until she found the card.

Thank you for your gesture of kindness.
My family and I will never forget your thoughtfulness.
May God bless you,
Grayson Sterling

Tracing her fingers over the handwritten, masculine script, she remembered the white rose casket spray she and Helen had lovingly put together. With no bill. She placed the card on top, closed the lid, and put the box away.

She checked the doors one more time and hurried to her car. The fuel gauge demanded her attention. Though she loved her hometown, it would be nice not to have to drive seven miles just to get gas.

As she entered Rose Bud, the cemetery beckoned. Not a living soul stirred. She pulled into the gravel parking lot.

The heavy iron gate groaned as she stepped through. With no clue where Grayson Sterling's wife was buried, Adrea strolled across the hardened earth covered with dormant yellowed grass. Indented graves interspersed with more recent, rounded mounds. Row upon row of aged, weather-beaten, and faded tombstones mingled with dust-spattered glossy newcomers.

A bird burst from a spindly bush. She pressed a hand to her heart. With a panicked beat of wings, the sparrow flew away.

Just as she was about to give up, she caught a glimpse of the white roses. They stood out among the other vibrant flowers and led her to a grave marked by a large, polished headstone.

Adrea remembered Sara's youthful beauty well, from the newspaper articles about the senseless hit-and-run accident that took her life. After running into the family left behind, seeing the cold marble monument brought the tragedy into sharp focus once again.

With a shiver, she read the epitaph: BELOVED DAUGHTER, WIFE, MOTHER: GONE TO MEET JESUS.

At least Grayson Sterling knew where to seek comfort for his grief. With a heavy heart, for someone besides herself for a change, she trudged back to her car.

A profound thought wrenched her gut.

"God, are You shoving him in my face to show me something? That's it. You're showing me that he's lost more than I ever thought about losing and he's going on, preaching Your sermons and raising his son—while I wrap myself in self-pity and bitterness, coveting other people's weddings. I lost a man I didn't need. A man who couldn't be faithful and couldn't be strong enough to beat the bottle."

She dropped to her knees on the cold ground.

"Oh, Lord, forgive me for my selfishness and be with Wade. He needs You to help him get sober again. He knows You, Lord. Help him to let You reintroduce Yourself." As she prayed for the man who'd broken her heart, the bitterness melted away. Forgiveness settled in her soul. A forgiveness she hadn't realized she needed to give. "Thank You, Lord. Thank You."

Before standing she added, "And, Lord, please be with Grayson and his little boy. Their world shattered two years ago, and I know they're still suffering. Give them comfort and strength, as only You can. Amen."

❧

Grayson turned into the driveway of a rambling, old, two-story house on the outskirts of Romance. He rechecked the address. It had to be the right place, but it certainly didn't look like apartments. Yet, there were several cars parked out front.

A large enclosed balcony gracing one entire side of the house erupted with flowers, despite the chilly winds of late February, while only a few potted plants or lawn chairs dotted the wrap-around porch. Must be divided into separate living quarters. A shame. He loved aged, spacious homes and hated seeing them cut up into apartments or converted into businesses.

A siren moaned in the distance. He took several deep breaths.

Stop being absurd. Every ambulance doesn't carry someone I love inside.

The siren drew close. Pressure welled in his chest, threatening

to burst through. The ambulance wailed past. He prayed. Relax...
inhale...exhale.

*Think. Sis is in the middle of catering a wedding. Dayne is at
Mom and Dad's house. None of them would be on the road right
now.* The pressure eased.

Regaining control, he sat a few minutes longer, then
stepped from the car.

Inside, he saw a long hallway with a door on each side and
a staircase in the middle. He climbed the steps, located the
right number, and rang the bell.

When the door barely opened, it wasn't a young seminary
graduate who greeted him. Instead, he peered through the
crack at a child.

"May I help you?" the little girl asked.

"Does Mark Welch live here?"

"Yes, but he's in the shower. You can wait if you want." She
started to close the door. "Sorry, but you're a stranger."

"That's true. I'm fine out here."

If only he could have gotten in touch with Mark. Moving
the meeting up, with someone he'd never met before, might
make Mark feel uncomfortable.

Within minutes, Grayson heard a male voice. The chain
released and the door opened. A man, his dark hair still
damp, beckoned him inside with a frown.

"She's out in the greenhouse." The man waved toward
glass doors. "I'd like to give you the third degree, but I have
to leave soon for an appointment. Count on it next time, if
there is a next time. For now, you're welcome to go on out.
Just watch yourself."

The man, presumably Mark, darted down the hall, leaving
Grayson no chance to explain his presence. Moments later,
the whir of a blow-dryer sounded from somewhere.

Unsure of what to do, he walked around the island,
separating the floral-themed living room from the sunny
yellow kitchen, toward patio doors. A woman knelt inside
the glassed-in balcony, surrounded by an explosion of colorful
blossoms.

She worked with the various plants, unaware of him. Potting soil streaked her red T-shirt and blue jean shorts, smudged her face, legs, and feet. With her long brunette hair pulled into a high ponytail and dirt everywhere, she was beautiful.

The splendor of the small, carefully tended garden came nowhere near the beauty of the woman in its midst. He studied her profile, the slight upward tilt of her small nose, the soft curve of her lips. Red polish adorned all twenty nails. Despite the grime, she exuded elegance.

Something familiar about her tugged at him. Adrea Welch. Of course, Mark and Adrea Welch. *Adrea Welch is beautiful—and married.* Grayson backed away from the door.

He didn't remember the deacons saying Mark was married with a child. He'd slogged through so many résumés they'd all begun to run together. And he'd never been detail oriented.

One detail stood out. Adrea was not available.

He shoved his hands into his pockets. *Great. I'm betraying my wife by finding this woman attractive and on top of that, she's married.*

The pressure started to build in his chest once more.

Why should I care if this woman is available? She's simply the florist. End of story.

His left temple throbbed.

Sara.

He'd never considered whether a woman was single or not—had never cared, even since his wife's death.

Bewildered and a bit frightened at such foreign thoughts, he considered leaving.

Adrea looked up and saw him.

Acting quickly, so she wouldn't realize he'd been watching her, Grayson opened the door. The moist potting soil mixed with the perfume emitted by dozens of different sweet-smelling flowers in the surprisingly warm room.

"Hello." Surprise reverberated in her tone. Her arched brows drew together. With the sun still peeking over the roof, she shielded her eyes to look up at him.

He forced words from his constricted throat. "Mark has

an appointment at the church with one of my deacons, who can't make it. I tried to call but didn't get an answer."

"You're here to interview him?"

"I decided to come and invite him to a casual lunch instead. I tried to let Mark know about the change in plans."

Adrea retrieved the cordless phone from a soil-strewn bench. "I guess the battery is low—or filled with grit."

Grayson concentrated on the flowers surrounding them. Greenhouse lights warmed pink orchids, white lilies, purple irises, and a whole host of others he couldn't identify.

The young girl, maybe a few years older than Dayne, sat on a redwood bench with a terra-cotta pot between her bare feet. Bent almost double, she planted bulbs. If only he'd noticed her before. She'd probably seen him watching Adrea.

"This is Haylee, my—"

"We already met." Haylee blushed. "I answered when I went in to get a drink." The little girl wagged a finger. "But I didn't undo the chain. I thought he was a stranger."

"And you acted appropriately." He smiled at the child, hoping to relieve her anxiety. "Mark told me I could wait out here." *In a roundabout way.*

"Why didn't you tell me someone was at the door, Haylee?" The girl shrugged. "He didn't ask for you."

Adrea patted the child's knee. "Next time, let me—"

The door slid open, and Mark popped his head out. "Yo, Adrea, I need help with my tie."

"Sure, I'm coming." She clapped her dirt-coated hands together and wiped them down the sides of her shorts. "Let's go inside, Haylee. We'll finish up here after Mark leaves."

Grayson stepped aside to allow Adrea and Haylee access.

Mark waited in the kitchen, dressed in a tan suit, his hair now dry.

"Don't come near me, Adrea. You're covered in grime."

"Don't worry, I'll be washed up in a minute."

"No time to wait." Mark paced the living room.

"Take deep breaths and I'll be right with you." She dashed to the sink.

In the adjoining living room, a Roadrunner cartoon transfixed Haylee.

"So, Mark, you graduated in December?" Grayson leaned against the dividing island.

"Yes." Mark frowned.

"I'm sorry, I tried to call—"

"Okay, let's see about that tie." Adrea returned, wiping her hands on a dish towel.

The smudges had disappeared from her face.

"Hurry, Adrea." Mark fidgeted.

She put her hands on his shoulders. "If you'd be still, I could tie it faster."

Grayson's insides squirmed as the intimate scene served up a painful reminder of him and Sara on a busy Sunday morning.

"You're not making a very good impression on Pastor Grayson." Adrea whispered in Mark's ear.

"Pastor Grayson?"

"Sorry, I never got around to introducing myself. I'm Grayson Sterling."

"You're the pastor?" Mark disentangled his tie from Adrea and turned around wide-eyed.

"Nice to meet you." Grayson offered his hand. "My deacon, Dr. Tom Deavers, got called to emergency surgery, so I decided to meet with you instead. I studied under Professor Cummings at seminary and he highly recommended you."

With a stiff handshake, Mark hung his head. "I'm so sorry, Pastor; I had no idea. I thought you were here to see Adrea."

Odd. What kind of man encourages his wife to have male visitors? She must meet with vendors for the floral shop at their home often, hence the comment about the third degree.

"No need to apologize." Despite his own discomfort, Grayson tried to put Mark at ease. "A simple misunderstanding."

"Let me finish." She moved in for another attempt with the tie.

"No need for the tie, either. I'm not wearing one. Relax. We're just two men of God, having a casual lunch together."

"It's nice of you to suggest Mark doesn't wear it, but if he takes off my hard work, I'll hurt him." She laughed, a melodious sound, and patted the tie. "There, all done."

Grayson shifted his weight from one foot to the other.

"Sorry I have to leave, Haylee, but we'll do something fun when I get back." Mark tousled the child's hair.

※

At the Rambler Café in Rose Bud, the waitress, with eyes full of sympathy, seated them at the corner table. She took their order and scurried to the kitchen. Grayson understood. Everyone felt sorry for him, whether they knew him or not. Sometimes he wished he could escape from the cloying compassion. He'd love to get away. Far away. To somewhere people didn't know what had happened. Away from the crushing weight of his grief.

Grayson surveyed the plank walls, the shelves above each window lined with plants, antique books, and plates. His gaze strayed to the table by the window. Nothing unique about it, just melamine with black chairs. His and Sara's table.

He took a sip of coffee. "All of the other applicants are from other states. I was hoping for someone local, so when I saw you studied under Dr. Cummings, then read his letter, I wanted to meet you."

Mark fiddled with his paper napkin. "Listen, back at the apartment. I'm sorry I thought you were there to see Adrea. She's had a rough time lately."

"No harm done." *What happened to her? Anything to do with the drunk?* "I need someone fast."

Mark's hands stilled, and his eyes met Grayson's.

Grayson shifted on the squeaky vinyl seat. "I'm having a hard time. Now."

"I'd really like to help you." Sincerity shone in Mark's gaze.

"For the past two years, I've gone through the motions." Grayson cleared his throat. "My pastoring skills have slipped. I'm running on empty, and I have a hard time focusing enough to study. My son needs me. I'm all he's got, and I'm afraid the church takes too much of me away from him. To be honest, I'm rethinking my decision to stay at Palisade."

Mark's jaw clenched. "I don't feel a call to pastor."

"That's not what I'm asking."

The waitress brought their drinks.

"I tried to convince the congregation they could get someone else. Someone, who wouldn't need an associate." Grayson sipped his sweet tea. "But they still want me to stay. If you take the position, you'll handle most of the evening services for a while, at least."

"I can do that." Mark squeezed a lemon slice into his ice water, ripped a blue packet open, and stirred its contents into his glass.

"Members of the congregation aren't telling me their problems, health issues, nothing." He looked out the window. A tractor putted along with a large, round hay bale on the fork. A convoy of vehicles followed. "Right now, I need to focus on Sunday morning and the pastoring part."

"I'm your man." Mark ran his finger around the rim of his glass. "A lot of associate pastors go into the field with the intention of moving up to senior pastor. Not me. I feel God called me to be a helpmate. To take the load off, in whatever area needed."

"Every time I tell God I'm quitting, He gives me a good kick in the backside. Maybe He's answering both our needs." Grayson swallowed hard. "Let's talk doctrine."

The waitress approached, her tray laden with food.

❧

While Adrea cleaned the already clean kitchen, Haylee finished watching the vintage cartoon DVD.

"Beep, beep." The Roadrunner outsmarted Wile E. Coyote once again.

Palisade had never had an associate and even when Mark told her they were looking into it, she didn't really think it would happen. Adrea had never expected Grayson's path to intersect with Mark's, much less have him appear on her balcony. All manners had flown from her head. She hadn't even asked if he wanted something to drink.

Why did Mark think he came to see me?

After the cartoon ended, they ate lunch and finished potting, then washed up. Adrea glanced at the clock.

Two hours had passed since Mark's departure. A nice jog in the park would be good about now. Jogging always burned nervous energy and made the time pass faster.

Mark's key clicked in the lock. He stepped inside, pulling his tie loose with a preoccupied look, revealing nothing.

"How did it go?" *Sound optimistic.*

"I don't know. We got off to such a bad start with my assuming he was here to see you. I should have known. I guess I was hoping you'd met someone."

"He stared at Adrea," Haylee said.

"He did? When?" Mark frowned.

"Before she saw him, when we were out on the balcony. I watched him, standing inside the door, staring at her."

With heart and mind racing, Adrea searched for an explanation. "I'm sure he was surprised to find me here. He's bought flowers from the shop for several years." She touched Mark's arm. "It wasn't a bad start. A little misunderstanding. No big deal."

The furnace clicked, then kicked on with a steady hum. "Yeah, but since I didn't realize who he was, I promised to give him the third degree in the future and sent him in your direction."

Adrea felt the warmth of a blush. "You weren't expecting your interviewer to show up here. I'm sure Grayson understood and thought the whole thing funny."

"It was kind of funny." Haylee giggled. "You should have seen the look on your face when you realized who he was."

"See?" Adrea poked Mark in the ribs. "Tell me about lunch."

"He just asked me doctrinal questions. At least we're on the same wavelength there."

"That's good. Listen, God will put you where He wants you, no matter how your interviews go. And this is probably only the first of many."

"In the meantime, let's go to Searcy. Maybe the roller rink." Mark raised an eyebrow. "Any takers?"

"Yay!" Haylee clapped her hands.

❧

Grayson stood at the kitchen sink, ever-present coffee cup to his lips. In the backyard, Dayne cavorted with Cocoa. Giggling and barks echoed. The dog had been a blessing and kept Dayne company.

The aged panes of glass needed the cracked caulking scraped away and reapplied. Maybe storm windows, too. The old house supplied endless projects. A good thing. Kept his mind busy.

The doorbell rang. "I'll get it." Grace laid the cone of white icing beside a cookie sheet lined with pastries.

Ginger and vanilla. Still warm. His hand hovered over a delicate cream puff. She'd know. She always knew.

"Ahem."

He turned to see Helen Fenwick in the doorway, holding a casserole dish with both hands.

"You didn't have to do this." A whiff of lasagna made his mouth water. "But I'm glad you did." He took the pan and set it on a hot pad on the counter.

"I heard Grace mention she had a wedding and a birthday today, so I knew she wouldn't have time to feed you and Dayne."

Her smile seemed forced.

"That's so thoughtful of you." Grace returned to her pastry decorating.

He pulled out a chair for Helen. "Sit down."

"I didn't come to stay. You eat your lunch while it's still hot."

"Only if you'll share it with me."

"Very well then." She sat. "Where's Dayne?"

"In the back with his dog." Grayson unwrapped the foil pouch on top of the lasagna dish to reveal garlic and butter steaming from the thick toast fresh from the oven.

"Okay, I'm done." Grace balanced several flat boxes on her hip. "Since you were so good at not stealing anything, I left you a few treats. Be back later."

"Bye, dear." Helen's eyelids looked puffy.

Grayson waited until they were alone. "Is everything all right, Helen?"

Moisture pooled in her blue eyes. "You have enough of your own problems."

"I'm your pastor." He handed her a tissue. "Please tell me what's wrong."

"It's Wade." She dabbed her eyes. "He's back in town."

"Is he drinking?" Helen had often asked for prayers on her alcoholic son's behalf.

"Yes. Off and on since his broken engagement a couple of years back."

"Why haven't you told me this?"

"I didn't want to burden you with anything else." Her hand trembled. "I shouldn't have told you now."

I have to pull myself together. The congregation—my congregation needs me.

"I was headed for the church after lunch. I'll wrap up a few things there and we can go talk with him, if you like."

She shook her head. "One of the deacons can help me with Wade."

"I've wanted to meet him anyway. Is he staying with you?"

"No. He's at some horrible motel-turned-apartments in Searcy, a good forty-five-minute drive."

An ominous chill crept down Grayson's spine. "I know where that is." *Basically, a drug house.*

❧

Adrea climbed the staircase two steps at a time, glad to be home after a long week at work. She loved the greenhouse with its private entry and her garden there. Yet, she longed for a real home instead of an old house with all its character slashed into four tiny apartments. A real yard, instead of a lot shared by all the tenants. . . A real place of her own.

She stepped around Mark's shoes in the middle of the floor. The apartment definitely felt more like a home with him there, even if he couldn't manage to pick up after himself.

"I'm home." No response. She checked the oven and announced louder, "I'm home."

"Yo, Adrea. It's about time." Mark's voice came from his room. "I'm starving."

His running joke, ever since they'd rented the first *Rocky* movie, always made her smile. "Is food all you ever think about?"

"When I'm hungry, it is."

Minutes later, Mark stepped up behind her in the kitchen. Adrea turned to tousle his hair.

"So did you hear anything from any churches?"

"Not yet." Mark plopped on the couch. "So you'd met Grayson Sterling before?"

Just the sound of his name made her pulse flutter.

"At the shop a few weeks ago and then we sort of ran into each other at the park." Adrea chose her favorite paring knife and sliced a tomato. The sharp blade cut clean lines through the soft pulp. "He's had a standing order for his wife for six years."

Until a hit-and-run driver carved his heart apart, just like the tender fruit in her hands.

"He still buys the flowers even though she died?"

A knot formed in her throat. "He takes them to the cemetery."

"Sad." Mark looked at the floor.

"He always comes to sign the card personally." She arranged the slices on a saucer. "The salesclerks call him Prince Sterling, and his four annual appearances are the highlights of every year."

"So, with all those visits to the shop, you never met him until a few weeks ago?"

Adrea shrugged. "I never work out front. So, what did you think of him?"

"Knowledgeable, compassionate. . . I could work with him."

"Maybe you will." *It's so nice to have him home, Lord.* In the few months since he'd graduated, he'd become so ensconced in her routine, it almost felt like he'd never left. *Please keep him close.* "God will work it out and put you exactly where He wants you."

"I forgot until I put this shirt on today." He pulled a small jewelry box from his shirt pocket. "I bought you something before I left Memphis."

"You didn't have to do that. How sweet." Finished with her task, she washed her hands and sat down beside him. She opened the gift to find a tiny ring with a pale yellow stone. "Oh, how pretty."

"It's a toe ring."

"I've never had one." Adrea stooped to her bare foot and slipped the ring on. "Is that the right place to wear it?"

"Beats me. Rachel will probably know. I got her and Haylee matching bracelets, but this made me think of you. Those toes need all the help they can get."

"Thank you. I love it, despite your tasteless remark." She threw the empty box at him.

He ducked. The phone rang and Mark grabbed it.

"Hello? Yes. It's good to hear from you. Really? When do you need an answer? Yes, I'll get back with you; and thank you."

"A church?"

"Palisade."

Her breath caught. Grayson's church. "Well, of course they want you. Why wouldn't they?" Palisade would keep him in Romance. She should be thrilled.

"It's a trial period. Interim type thing."

"When do you have to answer?"

"Couple of days. I better go do some praying."

She hugged him. "I'm so proud of you. First interview and you ace it."

&

Adrea turned into her parents' drive. Sam and Theo Welch sat in the porch swing, swaying slowly in the March breeze, both still trim and athletic. Mom's dark auburn hair remained without a trace of gray, with no help from her hairdresser. Daddy's thick mane had long ago turned silver; his rich brown eyes surrounded by laugh lines.

"Mark hasn't shown up for his own celebration dinner?" Adrea rolled her eyes.

"No and dinner's ready." Mom propped a hand on one hip.

A three-legged calico cat sat on the step.

"Hey, Tripod." At the sound of his name, he curled around Adrea's ankles. "Hey, boy, I missed you, too."

She picked Tripod up to scratch his special place along the side of his throat. He purred his appreciation. The long-ago abandoned cat had been her last rescued stray before she left home.

Only a kitten then, it seemed he was so grateful, he'd never put on "cattitude" airs. When Adrea called, he came, just like a dog. Now around seven years old, she longed to take him with her each time she left, but her landlord didn't allow pets.

Mark turned in and parked next to her car. She set Tripod down.

"Yo, Adrea. I'm starving."

"Imagine that." Mom swatted at him, then followed with a warm embrace. "Dinner's ready. Just waiting for you. The others are inside."

Adrea lagged behind to walk in with him. "You look tired."

"I've prayed over this decision more than I've slept lately."

"So since you have a job, do you think we could get a house one of these days?"

"A house, huh?" Mark laughed. "Palisade can't pay an associate that much. I'll probably have to do some counseling on the side. And besides, it's just an interim."

"Yes, but they'll love you."

"You always have such faith in me. Someday, you'll have a husband to buy a house with. All in God's timing."

A sigh escaped. "I'm fine, but not fine enough to go there."

Mark stopped on the porch and gently gripped her forearms. "I just want you to know, you're young, beautiful, and precious. Just because you fell for a jerk in disguise, your life isn't over. I know how much you want a family and I'm praying for your future."

She blinked away the sting of tears.

He kissed her forehead.

Rachel, her husband, Curt, and Haylee joined the procession to the kitchen.

The aroma of pork loin permeated the air. A dish Adrea hadn't mastered. While Mom's turned out moist and fork-tender, Adrea's attempts came out dry and the consistency of cardboard.

"Will you ask the blessing, Curt?" Daddy asked.

As the family bowed their heads, a symphony began to play on Adrea's cell phone. She grabbed it. An unfamiliar number appeared and she turned it off. All eyes were upon her.

"Sorry about that." Adrea turned the ringer off.

The doorbell rang.

"Who could that be?" Mom frowned.

"Y'all go ahead. I'll get it." Adrea jumped up, intent on ridding her family of interruptions.

As she swung the heavy oak door open, every nerve ending reverberated.

How could he have the nerve to come here, especially with Mark around? By the looks of him, Wade really didn't know what he was doing.

three

Stepping outside, Adrea quietly closed the door behind her. "Why are you here?"

"We really didn't get to talk the other day."

"No, I mean here." She pointed to the house.

"I wanted to see you. Mark said Mom—I mean." He shook his head, as if to clear it. "Mom said Mark was celebrating something, so I figured you'd be here."

He'd gotten his hair cut into his usual casually layered style, but dark, sunken circles still shadowed his ice-blue eyes. She'd once dreamed of their children with those eyes.

Without the bloodshot effect.

"Look." Her voice shook. "We're over. We have been for a long time."

The door opened and a glaring Mark stepped out. The veins in his neck looked ready to erupt. "What are you doing here?"

"I need to speak with Adrea." Wade's watery eyes pleaded with her.

"Well, she doesn't want to see you. Ever again. Do you understand?" Mark barked a derisive laugh. "I doubt it, you're so drunk you can't even slur straight."

"This doesn't concern you." With effort, Wade enunciated each word slowly and clearly. "This is between her and me."

Mark launched a fist.

"Mark! No!" Adrea grabbed for her brother's arm—too late.

Wade stumbled back, cupping his mouth. Blood dripped from between his fingers.

"Just go. Please." She squeezed her eyes shut. "We don't have anything left to say."

"What's going on?" Daddy stood in the doorway. "Wade?"

"Hello, sir." Wade tried to sound sober but failed. His voice wobbled and so did his stance. "I'd just like to talk to Adrea. Alone."

"You want more?" Mark raised his clenched fist again, white knuckled.

Daddy stepped between the younger men. "It's time for you to leave, Wade. Now."

Wade wiped his bleeding lower lip with the back of his hand. With one more pleading look at Adrea, he slunk to his black Escalade.

She could see another man in the driver's seat. Thankfully, Wade wasn't driving.

Mark flexed his blood-speckled knuckles.

Adrea couldn't tell if it was his or Wade's.

"Go clean up, without alerting your mother." Daddy pointed at Mark, using his best shame-on-you tone. "We'll talk about that temper of yours later. You could lose the interim job we're supposed to be celebrating over a stunt like that."

Her brother hung his head and went inside.

"Listen, Daddy, I know you're worried." Adrea hugged herself. "But I'm not stupid."

"Sweetheart, we don't think you're stupid." He put his arm around her, and they settled on the porch swing. "But, you're very sweet and softhearted. I just don't want you to get reeled into his web again."

"And I won't. I can't help Wade. The only one who can help him is God."

The door opened and Mom stuck her head out. "Hey, what's going on out here? The food's getting cold and I can't even seem to interest Mark in eating."

❧

Sunday morning dawned bright and beautiful, but Adrea's stomach flipped and flopped.

Mark drove past their church, in the middle of Romance, with its plain white block facade. Not known for its splendor, with out-of-date gold carpet and pews with no cushions, the church's charm dwelled in the warmth of its congregation.

From the time she could remember, her family had attended the small church of fifty or so faithful. When Pastor Frank retired, fiery young Curt came to town and promptly married their sister.

"Look, you really like Mountain Grove." Mark covered her hand with his. "Since I've been away, I got out of the habit of going to church with the folks. But you haven't. You don't have to do this."

"I want to. You know Mom and Dad would come, too, if they didn't teach classes." Adrea flipped down the mirror on the back of the visor and dabbed on mauve lipstick.

Palisade was in Rose Bud, eight miles farther from the apartment and quite large. Helen said the congregation numbered 150. Approximately, 148 strangers. And one all-too-familiar pastor.

With Mark at Palisade, she'd be more deeply drawn into the lives of the equally irresistible pastor and his son. *Maybe Mark won't get the position permanently.* She mentally kicked herself. *Palisade will keep Mark close. And keep me from being so lonely.*

As he pulled into the lot, the red brick exterior looked big and imposing.

"It means a lot that you're willing to support me."

She managed a brave smile. "Let's go."

They entered the church. Adrea surveyed the high wood ceiling. Deep burgundy carpet cushioned each footstep. The pews shone, freshly polished, with padded seats in an exact shade to match the plush floor. Every window boasted stained glass.

Just as pretty as she remembered from the last wedding she'd done there. Prettier than Mountain Grove.

Until recently, she'd never thought of where Mark's calling might lead—or realized she'd feel compelled to support him. And on top of everything else, there was her attraction to Grayson Sterling.

At the back of the sanctuary, Mark introduced Adrea to several people, with an impressive grasp of names and positions.

With his powerful sermons and charming, boyish personality the congregation would love him.

As she met several welcoming members, Adrea began to feel comfortable. Until she saw Grayson and Dayne. Her breath hitched.

With them, she saw a fresh-faced woman who looked as if she could go horseback riding at a moment's notice. *Strong resemblance. Must be Grayson's sister.*

Dayne ran to greet them. The adults followed.

"Hi, Adrea, I'm so glad you came to church." The boy grabbed her hand.

"Me, too. I hoped to see you this morning."

"Are you gonna come here all the time?"

"We'll just have to see."

A deacon pulled Mark aside as the adults caught up with the excited child.

Grayson began making introductions. "This is Grace, my twin. This is Adrea, the florist over in Romance."

"I've seen your lovely work at numerous weddings."

"You have?"

"I'm a caterer. Delectable Entrees. Is this your first visit to Palisade?"

"It is. I've always attended Mountain Grove, but as long as Mark is here, so am I."

As Mark rejoined the group, Grace turned to him. "Ah, the prospective associate pastor. My brother works entirely too hard. I hope you'll permanently take the position, along with some of his load." She extended her elegant hand.

"We'll have to see what everyone else thinks of me and how well I fit in."

"My sister, Grace," Grayson said. "This is Mark Welch, Adrea's husband."

At Adrea's sharp intake of breath, Mark tried to cover his laughter with a cough.

❧

Grayson cleared his throat.

"Well, I assumed you're married, since the two of you

live together." He knew of other churches lowering their standards to go along with the ways of the world, but not his church. He didn't know what else to say.

Surely, he hadn't contacted a young seminary graduate living with a woman out of wedlock. Surely, Dr. Cummings wouldn't have recommended such a candidate as a potential assistant pastor.

"Mark is my brother." Adrea blushed a pretty shade of pink.

"I apologize." A sigh escaped Grayson. *At least, I wasn't attracted to another man's wife.* "That day at the apartment, I just assumed. . . Who is Haylee?"

"Our niece."

"Well, I had a whole little family set up."

"What class do you plan to attend?"

Grace to the rescue. She tucked her hand in his elbow.

"What are the choices?" Mark asked.

"We have an adult, men only, women only, and a new singles class. I go to the adult. We're studying the writings of the apostle Paul."

"Sounds good to me." Mark grinned, looking ready to follow Grace anywhere.

"What about you, Adrea?" *Don't sound so anxious.*

"The adult is fine."

Her words made his heart beat faster. Though he tried not to look at her, she was even prettier in her yellow dress with high-heeled sandals and a matching ring just above the knuckle of the second toe of her left foot. Her nails were peach today.

The harpist began to trill a hymn.

Ready to flee Adrea's suddenly available presence, Grayson turned toward the stage. "I better get up there."

❧

After the closing prayer at the end of the service, Mark whispered, "Will you come stand with me as people leave? I'm kind of nervous."

Adrea's mouth went dry. One hundred forty-eight strangers.

She linked her arm through his. "People will think we're married."

"That was weird, huh?" Mark escorted her toward the back of the sanctuary. "So is Grace attached?"

"We're about to greet people and you're worried about getting a girlfriend."

He shot her a crooked grin.

The congregation began to scatter, and several people came to shake their hands as Pastor Grayson made introductions. While trying in vain to memorize names and faces, Adrea watched for Helen, hoping to get the chance to speak with her friend.

Ah, someone she knew. Jack Phillips. The mechanic/deacon wore permanent grease under his nails and taught the adult lesson this morning. Though Jack was a great teacher, Grayson's presence in the class distracted her. Jack introduced his family and the first group moved on. A break in the crowd lengthened.

"So is she?" Mark interrupted her thoughts.

Adrea had been too engrossed in memorizing to remember their discussion.

"Is who what?"

"Is Grace attached?"

"I don't think so. Seems like Helen told me awhile back that Grace moved in with Grayson and Dayne after Sara's death." *I mean, Pastor Grayson.*

"If Grace will agree to lunch, will you come with us?"

"Yes, now perform your duties before you get dismissed on your first day."

Soon Mark was in his element and Adrea knew he didn't need her hovering over him. She strolled outside to stand in the warm sunshine.

A few minutes later, Grace joined her. "So you plan to join us for lunch?"

"Yes, where are we going?"

"The guys said it's up to you and Mark."

"The guys?" The tiny butterflies in her stomach turned into luna moths.

"Dayne and Grayson are coming along."

Before Adrea could respond, Dayne stood at her elbow, bubbling with excitement. "We're going to Dexter's!"

Mark joined them. "The new pizza place in Searcy?"

"No, Dayne." Grayson shook his head. "We agreed that Mark and Adrea could pick."

"Why not Dexter's?" Mark asked. "I love that place."

Grace shielded her eyes from the sun. "They always have a dozen birthday parties happening all at once."

"It's loud." Grayson grimaced. "And not a good place for adult conversation."

"Who needs adult conversation?" At a kid-centered place, she could avoid Pastor Grayson. "I love their pizza."

"Pizza is my favorite." Mark's childlike glee melted Adrea's uneasiness into a smile.

Grace raised elegant fingertips to her temple. "It's the noisiest place on earth and gets on most adults' nerves."

Despite her no-frills look, with minimal makeup and straight, long hair, Grace's nails modeled a flawless French manicure.

"Who said we're adults?" Mark grinned at Grace.

Adrea could tell he was smitten from his dopey gaze.

"Can they ride with us?" Dayne asked.

"Let's take my car, so we can all fit." Grace motioned toward a white sedan. "That is if you don't mind Dayne's booster seat."

"Adrea, hello."

She turned to see Helen, with red-rimmed eyes and perfectly coifed hair to match her slate dress. "I looked for you all morning."

"I'm so glad you and Mark will be here." Always free with hugs, she embraced Adrea.

"Me, too."

"Pastor, could I speak with you and the new associate?" a young man asked.

Grayson and Mark stepped away.

"Come on, Dayne." Grace took the boy's hand. "We'll wait in the car."

Adrea touched the older woman's arm. "Are you okay?"

"The usual. Half the time Wade doesn't answer when I call." Helen's chin trembled. "He should have stayed in Missouri. Away from that girl."

Adrea patted her hand. "Maybe we can check on him this week."

"You're such a dear. So, you're going to lunch with Pastor Grayson?"

"He and Grace invited both Mark and me."

"You and Mark will fit in perfectly here." She glanced over Adrea's shoulder. "I think the pastor's ready."

The two women hugged again, and Adrea turned to see Grayson waiting a few yards away. He matched his stride to hers as everyone else headed for their cars.

"Adrea, sit in the back with me." Dayne patted the seat.

Mark was already up front with Grace, while Grayson, Dayne, and Adrea sat in the back. Just like a family.

The usual commotion of Dexter's dispelled Adrea's niggling discomfort. She counted eight birthday parties in progress. Laughter, excited voices, and numerous festive horns echoed around them.

Dayne dragged Adrea from one video game to the next, soundly beating her at each until their order arrived, served by a clown on Rollerblades.

Mark blessed the food.

Though the gleeful squeals of delight surrounding the group forced them to speak loudly, the adults managed to carry on a conversation. Pastor Grayson and Mark discussed the month trial period and then a membership vote.

"It's really my decision, but I like the congregation to have their say in such an important step." Grayson served Dayne a second piece of pizza. "After all, Palisade has never had an associate before."

"I can't hear half of what you're saying." Grace leaned closer. "This really isn't a good place for discussion."

"Why don't you all join us for lunch next Sunday?" Mark sipped his water-turned-lemonade. "At our place. After

Adrea graduated high school and we got the apartment together, she was a horrible cook. That's partly why I decided to go to seminary."

Adrea's breath caught. Not another lunch with Pastor Grayson. She elbowed her brother in the ribs.

"Ow! You didn't let me finish. Much to my relief, her culinary skills have greatly improved."

"That's nice of you to ask." Grayson shot a well-mannered look toward Adrea. "But maybe you should check with your sister on this. She may not want to cook for five people."

"I don't mind at all." *Didn't sound very convincing.* She pasted a smile on her face. "I just didn't like Mark advertising my once dismal cooking. Please come."

Grace folded her napkin. "Can I bring something?"

"Just yourself. Oh my. One of my invited lunch guests is the best caterer in town. Now, I'm nervous."

"Don't be ridiculous. Anything you fix will be great."

"You know"—Mark grinned—"I was just kidding about the decision to go to seminary."

Adrea jabbed him again.

"Ow!"

After the meal, the men disagreed over who would pay the ticket. The restaurant had cleared of the after-church crowd and only the birthday partiers remained, with children on a giddy sugar high. Seeking peacefulness, Adrea stepped outside to wait.

"Yo, Adrea." Mark slung his arm around her shoulders. "I guess I should have asked you first, but I got caught up in the moment. Want me to cancel?"

"Of course not. It's fine."

"We could have it catered. Hey! We could get Grace to cater our lunch."

"That would be great. 'Would you join us for lunch and can you bring the food, too?'" Adrea laughed. "Don't worry, I really don't mind. It'll be fun."

Fun? An afternoon spent trying not to eyeball the great-looking preacher with even more emotional baggage than me.

Since Helen's visit, Grayson had tried to catch up with Wade, but Adrea's distress call surprised him.

He pulled into the lot of the rundown motel-turned-apartment-complex. Mildewed concrete blocks with peeling white paint trimmed in a neon lime color. Adrea's silver G5 sat next to Wade's Escalade.

How much longer could Wade afford his fancy ride? Helen said he hadn't worked since he'd come to town.

Grayson's deacon, Jack Phillips, parked beside him, and they headed toward the building.

"Nice place," Jack deadpanned.

"Yeah. Look, I'm not sure what we'll find here. Wade is an alcoholic. Adrea brought Helen to check on him. He's drunk and she's upset."

"I'm prepared. My uncle was a drunk."

They climbed the rusty iron steps to the second level and Grayson knocked on the door. "Wade."

The door opened.

Adrea greeted them with worry-filled eyes, holding a trash bag. "I shouldn't have brought her here. I didn't know who else to call." She gestured to a doorway.

Dreading what he might find, he crossed the living room, followed by Jack. The smell of garbage greeted them. Grayson's stomach turned.

Helen sat by the bed. Splayed across the sheetless mattress, in a grungy T-shirt and shorts, Wade looked dead. His oily hair matted to his head, and dark circles under his eyes told the tale—along with the whiskey bottle on the floor. He looked familiar. The drunk from the florist shop. This was Wade Fenwick?

Empty fast-food containers lined every available surface, and flies buzzed from one rotting morsel to the next. Wadded clothes, remote controls, and beer cans strewn across the floor created an obstacle course. Grayson traversed the refuse.

"Helen?"

The older woman whirled around. "Oh, Pastor Grayson.

Jack." Her face crumpled. "What do we do now?"

Grayson put a comforting hand on her shoulder. "We could try to convince him to go back into rehab."

"He's been too many times to count." Her watery voice wobbled.

"What about Mission 3:16?"

"You know, I don't think he's ever been in a Christian facility." Helen wrung her hands.

Wade stirred and slowly opened his eyes. "Adrea? Don't leave me," he muttered.

four

Grayson frowned. "Hello, Wade. I'm your mother's pastor, Grayson Sterling."

Unfocused eyes widened. "No. It can't be. I'm dreaming again? How did you find out?"

"Just calm down, Wade," Grayson spoke slowly, as if to a simpleton. "Your mom is here, and this is Deacon Jack Phillips."

"I'm sorry. I didn't mean to hurt anyone."

The distraught man lost consciousness again.

"What's he talking about?" Jack whispered.

"He must be hallucinating. I'll call the mission and see if they can help." He turned toward Adrea, who was still picking up trash in the living room. "Take Helen home. Jack and I will handle things from here."

Adrea nodded. The haunted look in her eyes reflected the depths of her soul.

She'd worked for Helen and he could see the two women were close, but why would Wade call out for Adrea in his drunken stupor?

That morning at the shop, he'd hoped Wade was just a drunk wandering the streets, harassing anyone who left their doors open. Could Adrea be in a relationship with Wade?

❦

Feeling shaky, Adrea climbed the stairs to the private balcony of her apartment.

What would Grayson think of her if he knew she'd caused Wade, an alcoholic, to go back to drinking? Had Wade said anything incriminating today?

Mark sat with his feet propped on the coffee table, reading his Bible. So serene. Nothing like the day she'd had.

She unlocked the sliding glass door, threw her keys on the

49

cheap melamine counter, and walked around to plop beside him, striving for casual.

He frowned. "Yo, Adrea. You okay?"

"Just peachy." Her stomach knotted tighter.

"How's Helen?"

"Worried about Wade."

"You're not getting involved, are you?"

"I'm just trying to support her. She called before I left the shop. She put Wade in a Christian rehab center today."

"Grayson told me about it. He said you took Helen to Wade's apartment."

"I didn't want her to go alone. I'm involved for Helen's sake. Not Wade's."

"Poor Helen." Mark shook his head, satisfied with her explanation. "I get the feeling you're uncomfortable around Grayson."

"Why would I be?"

"You tell me."

Mark knew her so well.

Adrea took a deep breath, debating on how much to tell him. No matter how hard she tried to relegate Grayson to the back of her mind, he remained at the forefront. She replayed each conversation they had, each time she saw him, again and again in her mind. Like a teenager.

"You'll think I'm silly."

"Just tell me, Adrea. I've never thought you were silly a day in your life, even when you were probably really silly. You've got a crush on him."

She shrugged. "Guess so. Now you think I'm silly, don't you?"

"Absolutely not, because I have a crush on his sister. Apparently the Sterlings are irresistible to the Welches."

"The thing is, Grace is available and she seems to like you, too."

"So Grayson likes you. What's the problem?"

"He's still in love with his wife." She propped her feet next to his. "It's only been two years."

"Two years is a long time. Maybe he's ready to move on."

"Trust me, he's not. Whenever he mentions her, fresh pain

snuffs out the sparkle in his eyes."

"Ooh." Mark winced. "You've got it bad. I hadn't noticed a sparkle in his eyes."

Adrea's face warmed. She elbowed him. "Two years is a long time, but not when a couple shared a love like he and Sara apparently did. Just trust me, Grayson Sterling is not available. And the last thing I need is another troubled man on my hands."

"He does have his share of baggage." Mark frowned. "Should my interim become permanent, we'll have to socialize with him. Would you rather I back out of this church and try somewhere else?"

"Don't you dare! You let God make the call. So, the church may make Grayson an indelible fixture in our lives. I'll just have to get used to his presence."

≈

Saturday afternoon, Adrea borrowed Haylee for a walk in the park. Daffodils nodded in the gentle breeze. A few families dotted the landscape with children and various-sized dogs scurrying about.

Haylee ran ahead, with ginger pigtails flying and long, coltish legs flailing. So similar to her mother at that age. Bright sunshine made it warmer than she'd expected, and Adrea wished she'd packed a lunch.

"So you're not coming to Mountain Grove again tomorrow?" Haylee asked as Adrea caught up.

"Mark really needs me to support him." Adrea tugged a pigtail. "It's like when you have to read a book report in front of the class; it helps to see a friendly face or two in the crowd."

"So he's preaching the morning service, but couldn't you come to nighttime church with us?"

"It would seem weird if I only went when he preaches."

As they walked across the crisp grass, something large crashed into the back of Adrea's legs, knocking her off kilter. She screamed.

Strong hands on each shoulder helped to restore her balance.

"Sorry about that," a familiar voice apologized. "I guess Cocoa remembers you."

She turned to see Grayson and Dayne, with Cocoa straining at his leash.

What did Wade say in his sometime conscious state? *Does he know about Wade and me?*

"With my bum knee, I can't hold him back when he goes full throttle."

Grayson didn't act any differently toward her.

Adrea stroked Cocoa's chocolate fur and turned to Haylee. "This is Cocoa and Pastor Grayson's son, Dayne."

The calmness of her own voice surprised her. For some reason her heart was about to beat out of her chest. *Must be adrenaline.*

"Hey." Dayne waved.

"Hello." Haylee responded with a shy grin.

"It's nice to see you again, Haylee." Grayson winked.

"Daddy, I'm hungry." Dayne kicked a pebble off the sidewalk. "Can Haylee and Adrea come on our picnic?"

"It's nice of you to invite us, but your father probably only packed for two." Adrea wrapped her arms around Cocoa's neck. "You go and we'll keep Cocoa company, if you don't mind. I promise not to let go of his leash."

"I can't let him drag you across the park." Grayson smiled, devastatingly unaware of his own attractiveness. "Grace packed enough for an army. Unless you have plans?"

Lunch with the drop-dead gorgeous preacher. *Might as well get to know my brother's earthly boss. Maybe put in a good word for Mark.*

"Actually, we're on our own today. I left Mark at home to do his Bible study in peace."

"I knew I liked him. He's studying while I hang out in the park."

Bingo. "Mark was so worried when his interview got off to such a confusing start."

Grayson laughed. "As I told Mark, our initial meeting convinced me he was the perfect candidate for associate pastor.

I wanted a human being, not some stuffed shirt. His down-to-earth personality, much prayer, and the recommendation from Dr. Cummings made the decision for me. I'm anxious to hear his sermon."

"Me, too." A dog barked, followed by the excited shout of a child. Cocoa's ears perked up.

"In the meantime, you ladies can help us pick a spot for our meal, since Dayne and I can never agree."

"On the way here, I wished we'd packed a lunch." Adrea looked across the park. "How about that big sycamore over there by the swings?"

"That's where I picked." Dayne jumped up and down. "Two against one, let's go!"

She expected the excited boy to run ahead, but he remained close by his father's side. Apparently, Grayson's warnings, after Cocoa chased the squirrel, had worked.

As Adrea helped spread the blanket, Haylee stayed close by and Dayne dug through the wicker basket.

"I don't believe I've ever seen a real red and white checkered picnic blanket." Adrea sat with her ankles crisscrossed and ran her hands over the soft fabric. "It's beautiful."

"Sara made it." His eyes dimmed.

"My favorite." Dayne removed a container from the basket and repeated the statement with each subsequent find.

With the contents emptied, Grayson blessed the food.

The chicken salad sandwiches beat Adrea's favorite deli.

Dayne carefully tore the crust of his sandwich away and fed it to Cocoa. The large dog waited patiently for an offering, then took each bite delicately between his teeth, careful not to nip his beloved owner.

"This is delicious." Unsnapped jeans would feel good about now.

"I'll tell Grace. She's the most sought-after caterer in town." Pride echoed in his voice.

"So she's working today, while we enjoy her mouthwatering food."

"Trust me. She wouldn't have it any other way."

Dayne and Haylee hurriedly finished their meals and ran to swing nearby. The young girl had finally warmed to the little boy.

"I'm glad the kids are having fun." Grayson watched Haylee push Dayne higher and higher.

"She's painfully shy. As a kid, I was the same way."

"Really? You don't seem shy now."

"I'm better than I used to be." Warmth crept up her cheeks. "For my first three months at the shop, Helen put me in the showroom. It was torture. Eventually, I realized I was more uncomfortable *not* talking to the customers than I was while attempting to make conversation. I still tend to clam up when I'm out of my element." *Or get nervous and prattle. Like now.*

"So, that's why I never met you. You hole up in the back and play with flowers." Several birds landed in the tree above. Grayson flinched.

"Is something wrong?" Adrea asked.

"On one of our first dates, I took Sara on a picnic and a bird decided to relieve itself—on my head."

Adrea tried to stifle her laughter but failed. "What did you do?"

"Sara always had a very weak stomach, so she threw up, cleaned me up, and we ate. That's when I knew she was the girl for me." He looked off in the distance, lost in memories. "I try to avoid trees."

The deep timbre of Grayson's voice cast a spell on her. He smiled, which deepened the crinkles at the corners of his eyes. Her fingers tingled to smooth away the lines of worry and grief. The sable lock of hair playing across his forehead in the mid-March breeze gave her the urge to brush it back from his brow.

Concentrate on something else. Anything but him. She noticed an ant, threading its way through the grass, struggling to carry a bread crumb Cocoa had missed.

"Daddy, I don't feel so good."

She looked up in time to see Dayne throw up.

Adrea's heart tumbled for the sobbing boy.

Sympathetic with her new friend's plight, Haylee patted his back.

Ineffectively, Grayson tried to clean the boy's face with a dry paper towel.

"I'll get wipes." Adrea jogged toward her nearby car.

Grabbing the towelettes, she ran back to the still sobbing boy and began washing his face and neck.

Grayson pressed his hand against Dayne's forehead. "You don't feel warm. You probably ate too fast and then played too hard. I should have made you wait and digest longer."

"We'll get you cleaned up in no time." She tried to assure the child while working on his shirt, then turned to his father. "Does he have extra clothes?"

"Actually, we picked up some fresh laundry from Mom's this morning." He flashed a sheepish grin. "She does our ironing."

"Do we have to go home, Daddy?"

"I'll get you another shirt. We'll stay for a while, but if you feel sick again, we'll have to leave." Grayson went to his car.

Adrea had the boy cleaned up by the time his father returned. Always the first to hurl at the sight of anyone tossing their cookies, it amazed her that the incident didn't sicken her. Instead, she simply dealt with the problem.

"Since Dayne seems fine now, I think we'll go." She threw their trash away.

"I doubt it's anything contagious. He got his weak stomach from Sara."

"If it's a virus, we've probably already been exposed. It's not that. Mark will wonder about us. And speaking of ironing, I do his shirts."

A dog yapped. Cocoa raised his ears and stared off in the distance. Following his gaze, Adrea saw a golden retriever lunge into the air to catch a neon orange Frisbee.

"Thanks for helping with Dayne. Seems like every time we're distressed in the park, you show up to save the day."

"No problem." Adrea smiled. "Thanks for letting us crash

your lunch. Please tell Grace how much we enjoyed her delicious meal."

"Don't go." Dayne grabbed Adrea's hand.

"We have to go home, but I liked having a picnic with you."

"Even though I threw up?"

"Well, I wish that hadn't happened, for your sake, but it didn't bother me."

"One time my Sunday school teacher threw up because a boy in class did."

Grayson scrunched his nose. "We don't need the details. Tell Adrea and Haylee good-bye."

"Bye, Adrea, bye, Haylee. I'm glad you came today."

"We are, too." Just how glad, Adrea didn't want to think about. She patted Cocoa on the head, then regretfully steered Haylee to the car.

"See you tomorrow," Grayson called.

⁂

Grayson paced the kitchen floor. Grace should have been home by now. Numerous times, he'd called her cell and gotten no answer. His heart thudded in his chest. He couldn't get enough air in his lungs. Not again. It couldn't happen again.

He closed his eyes and the memories swirled. Sara looked so peaceful by the glow of the dash light. With her seat tilted back a bit, she fell asleep. The slightly wilted white rose lay in her lap.

In his rearview mirror, he could see Dayne curled to the side in his car seat, with one arm flung over his face.

Grayson stopped at the four-way, looked both ways, and continued. A flash of light to his right. The impact hurled the car sideways. A white explosion hit him in the face, the car spun, metal tore, glass crunched. The car slammed into something solid and came to an abrupt halt. His right knee jammed into the steering column. His scream mixed with cries from the backseat.

Sara was silent.

He shook the images away and took several deep breaths.

Willing his fumbling fingers to work, he dialed the hospital. Just as it rang, the back door opened. Grace. Marvelous, healthy, all in one piece, Grace. He hung up.

"Where have you been?" He rushed toward her with a hug.

"Can't breathe," Grace whispered.

He eased up but couldn't bring himself to let go. "You're late." His voice broke on a sob.

"Oh, Grayson." She rubbed her palms over his back in soothing circles. "I told you I had a big luncheon today. It went longer than I planned."

"I tried to call." *At least twenty times.*

"My cell needs charged. I'm so sorry I worried you."

Steeling his resolve, he pulled himself together and let her go. He sank to a chair.

She touched his cheek, her eyes bright with tears. "You can't go on like this."

"I'm okay. Really." He wiped his face with a paper napkin. The wooden legs of his chair scraped against the tile floor as he scooted closer to the table. He leaned his elbows on the surface, his face in his hands.

"Maybe a counselor would help. Mark does counseling on the side."

"I have the best counselor in all of heaven. I'm fine. Just call me next time."

"I promise. And I'll make sure my cell is charged, so I can leave it on vibrate."

"How did your luncheon go?"

"Great. Several people asked for my card." She opened the cabinet and got a glass. "So, what did you do today, other than almost have a coronary over nothing?"

"Dayne and I had a picnic in the park."

"Oh good." Ice clinked into the glass she held under the dispenser. "Quality time."

"That, too, but we actually ran into Adrea and her niece, so Dayne invited them to join us."

"Where was Mark?"

"Home studying. They loved your sandwiches."

"Good thing I sent extra." Grace filled her glass with ice water and took a sip. "So, Adrea's very pretty and seems really sweet."

Grayson cleared his throat.

"I'll take it you agree."

Something in his chest boiled. "It wasn't like a date or anything."

"I didn't say it was."

"We had a picnic in a very public place with two kids." He stormed out of the kitchen.

She followed. "Grayson, you know Sara would want you to move on. To be happy."

He took the stairs two at a time.

⁂

Saturday evening, Mom and Dad stopped by the apartment.

Adrea tried not to fidget as Mom surveyed her from hair to toenail.

"You're too thin." Mom tapped her chin with a forefinger.

"I weigh the same as the last time you saw me." Adrea hugged her mother, who weighed only slightly more. Somehow, Mom always wanted to fatten her up.

"You're taller than I am. You need some meat on your bones. Men don't like beanpoles. Isn't that right, dear?"

"Yes, dear," Daddy said.

"Daddy, you're supposed to be on my side."

"Sorry, sweetness, after thirty years, I've learned to just agree with your mother. It keeps the peace."

Mom playfully swatted at her husband. "I thought you might need help with tomorrow's lunch."

Adrea lifted the lid off the slow-cooker. The brisket bubbled with floating potatoes and carrots.

"Smells like everything's under control." Mom settled on the floral sofa beside Daddy. "So, Adrea, are there any candidates on the horizon? Surely a big ole church like Palisade has plenty of eligible bachelors."

"There are no candidates." Adrea straightened the magazines on the coffee table. "Besides, candidates are in politics. Why don't you bother Mark about women? He has a thing for Grace Sterling."

"I already told her." Mark flashed a beat-you-to-it grin.

"Tell me about him?" Mom prompted.

"There's no him." Adrea fluffed a throw pillow and sat beside their dad.

Unsatisfied, Mom turned to her son. "Mark?"

"There are a few sparks flying between Adrea and my potential new pastor."

"There are not." Adrea hurled the pillow at her brother.

He caught it.

"Grayson Sterling?" Mom smiled at the possibilities.

Mark nodded. "Adrea calls him Prince Sterling."

"I do not!" Adrea jumped up.

"I always knew you'd make a perfect preacher's wife." Their mother clasped her hands together as if in prayer.

"Mother!" Adrea propped both hands on her hips. "Mark, I'm never speaking to you again. There are no sparks."

"You're protesting too much, dear. Ooh, and a twin. I might just get twin grandbabies."

"Mother!"

"Tell me more, Mark." Mom patted the seat beside her.

"When I first met Grayson, he assumed Adrea and I were married." Mark chuckled. "He even thought Haylee was our daughter. When he learned different, I've never seen such relief on a man's face."

Incapable of stopping the conjecture, Adrea rolled her eyes heavenward and left them to it. "I'll go iron Mark's shirt."

A few minutes later, as Adrea and the iron steamed, Mom entered the room.

She perched on the edge of Adrea's yellow satin and lace comforter. "So Grayson sounds wonderful."

"He is, but he's still in love with his wife. She's only been gone two years."

"Well, he can't go it alone forever. He's a young man. His son needs a mother."

"You may be right." Adrea sighed. "But I don't feel up to

the challenge of getting a man to move forward from his past. I tried that with Wade."

"Sorry I brought it up. You know I just want you to be happy." Mom touched her hand. "We're leaving. Turn the slow-cooker down soon, or the meat won't be tender."

❧

After class, Adrea waited on the steps of the church until their parents caught up.

Mark stood with Grayson at the entrance to the sanctuary. "Mom, Dad, I'd like you to meet Pastor Grayson Sterling. This is his son, Dayne, and his sister, Grace. Everyone, our parents, Theodore and Samantha Welch."

"Call me, Sam." Mom surveyed the stained-glass windows lining the sanctuary with a rainbow of color bursting on the white walls.

"And I'm just Theo."

"It's a pleasure to meet both of you," Grayson said as Daddy pumped his arm. "I'm glad you could join us for the service."

"We wouldn't miss Mark's first official sermon at Palisade." Mom hugged Grace a little too eagerly.

Mark winced.

Adrea stifled laughter.

"Go ahead; put the pressure on, Mom. It's not like I wasn't nervous already."

"You'll be fine." Mom kissed his cheek, imprinting him with her trademark fuchsia shade. "I've been praying for you."

Branded many times before, Mark wiped the smear away with his handkerchief as Rachel and Haylee arrived.

"I didn't know y'all were coming!" Mark hugged them.

"I wanted to surprise you. I couldn't miss my brother's first official sermon."

The harpist began a hymn.

"Thanks, sis. It means a lot to me. I better get up there."

Everyone found seats.

The congregation sang; then Mark took the pulpit, obviously ready to launch into his sermon.

"Ephesians 3:17–19 says, 'That Christ may dwell in your hearts by faith; that ye, being rooted and grounded in love, may be able to comprehend with all saints what is the breadth, and length, and depth, and height; and to know the love of Christ, which passeth knowledge, that ye might be filled with all the fulness of God.'"

Several amens echoed.

Mark flipped back toward the Old Testament, Bible pages rustling. "Now turn to Isaiah 53:5, 'But he was wounded for our transgressions, he was bruised for our iniquities: the chastisement of our peace was upon him; and with his stripes we are healed.'"

Adrea's eyes welled with tears several times during the service. Mark's sermon demonstrated how deeply Jesus loves us. Enough to leave His heavenly home and come to live among us, knowing He would be savagely beaten and killed.

When the altar call came, she went to thank God for sending His Son to save her soul and Jesus for enduring the punishment for her sins. It made her dilemmas seem so trivial.

She memorized a few more members of the large congregation. Red hair, nosy, Sylvie Kroft. No husband, at least no one mentioned him. Gray hair, slightly stooped over, Mrs. Jones, kind, forced smiles. Tom Deavers, the deacon/doctor with a handshake so firm, her fingers ached afterward. His wife, Patty; sons Tommy, Timmy, and Terry. She only saw Helen in passing. The older woman seemed a bit more at peace. Maybe Wade's treatment was going well.

❧

When she and Mark arrived at the apartment, a mix of smells permeated the kitchen. Succulent beef brisket and the perfume of flowers, from her garden and the shop, filled the air creating a captivating aroma. Their parents arrived in time for Daddy to help Mark put both leaves in the table and round up every seat they owned, even a couple of lawn chairs.

Just as Adrea took their dessert from the oven, the Sterlings arrived, followed by Curt, Rachel, and Haylee.

"I'd like to offer my help." Grayson leaned against the counter. "But I'm useless in the kitchen."

"I'll help." Grace stepped around the dividing island.

"There's not much left to do other than put ice in the glasses." With trembling hands, Adrea set the final plate on the wall-to-wall table. "And, Grace, you do this sort of thing all the time. You are taking this day off."

"I can handle ice." Grayson grabbed a glass and Adrea heard clinking.

With the table ready, Mark said the prayer and they all took their seats.

"So, how's the church?" Curt passed the rolls.

"I love Palisade. The people are wonderful. I only wish. . ."

Adrea watched Grayson mentally leave, though he sat at their table with his glass of sweet tea halfway to his lips. Conversation stalled as everyone waited for his return and he snapped out of the memory.

"Sara always loved this area. In fact, we were married at Mountain Grove. My typical bride wanted her wedding in Romance."

"She'd be proud of you." Mom patted his arm.

"Mrs. Fenwick is definitely proud." Daddy passed the brisket. "She was singing your praises to everyone she saw."

"Dear Helen. I'm afraid I haven't always been there for her." A shadow passed over his face. He glanced at Dayne. "Adrea, this is one of the best meals I've had that my sister didn't cook."

Her face warmed. She gestured toward her mother. "Mom helped."

"I didn't do a thing." Mom, a firm believer that the way to a man's heart is through his stomach, grasped the opportunity to plug Adrea's cooking. "Adrea had it all prepared before our arrival."

"But Mom taught me how."

"A bit belatedly," Mark said. "Ow! Adrea, you have the boniest elbows."

Laughter followed the exchange.

After the meal, the children ran to play outside. Mark and Grace insisted on helping Adrea clean up, but Grayson managed to shoo them away to supervise the kids. Traitors, her parents, Rachel, and Curt disappeared also.

Alone with the man of her dreams. A man who still loved his deceased wife.

"How does Mark like the church?" Grayson gathered the plates while Adrea loaded them.

She turned on the dishwasher. "He loves it."

"What about you? What do you think of Palisade?"

"At first, the size intimidated me, but I'm getting used to it. However, it'll take me quite some time to learn everyone's name." She set the yellow quilted place mats back on the table.

Grayson wiped the countertops. "Don't worry, you'll get to know them all. They'll make sure of it. If anything can be said of the people at Palisade, they're very friendly. Once they get to know you, you'll get hugs instead of handshakes."

"I'm already getting a few."

Finished with the counters, Grayson leaned against the refrigerator.

She could feel him watching her.

"Mark did a great job on the sermon this morning."

"Did you really think so?" Her voice quivered.

"Of course, didn't you?"

The steady hum of the dishwasher, followed with a gurgle, and the clunk of two plates together filled the pause.

"I thought he was awesome. I just wondered if you really thought so or if you were simply being nice."

"If I didn't truly enjoy the sermon, I wouldn't say anything."

"I'm so proud of him."

Grayson pulled out a chair and sat.

Though she'd hoped to escape his presence, Adrea followed suit and claimed the seat across from him.

"He's got my vote and the congregation seems to like him, as well. With Mark to rely on, I can focus better on what I need to do."

"It was only one sermon. Let's not get ahead of ourselves." Adrea decided to broach the issue on her mind. "I'm thinking about trying the women's class for a few weeks. And if Mark were to stay at Palisade, I heard the kindergarten/first grade class needs a teacher. I used to teach children at Mountain Grove and really enjoyed it, but I stepped aside to let a newer member have a chance."

The dishwasher stopped between cycles. *Drip, drip, drip.* The steady beat on the stainless-steel sink punctuated the silence.

His jaw twitched. "You'll do anything to get away from me." His teasing tone sounded forced.

Adrea felt the blush creep across her cheeks. She hoped he was unaware of how close he was to the truth. She stood and turned the faucet handle until the drip stopped then reclaimed her seat.

"No, really, you should attend whichever class you feel you'll get the most from. So, you've given me another reason to vote Mark in." Grayson fiddled with the lace edging on a place mat. "Sara used to teach that class."

"I'm sorry. I didn't mean—"

He held up a hand. "It's okay. We have to move on. Since Mrs. Roberts' illness, Mrs. Jones has filled in. She's good with the kids, but since her husband passed, she's been distracted. The kids need some consistency."

"I'll pray about it."

"It's nice to have people willing to volunteer." He cupped his chin between forefinger and thumb, then propped his elbow on the table. "You and Mark fit in well. That's one of my favorite things about Palisade. Everyone pitches in to help. I've seen churches where the same five people do all the work while the rest of the congregation sits and warms their pews or, even worse, complains about the way things are done."

"I like to do my part." Adrea straightened the salt and pepper shakers in a nice line. "Though my time seems to become more and more limited. I thought owning the florist shop would allow me to set my hours, maybe work only three days a week. Instead, I work five and most weekends." *And I'll probably spend them running into you at weddings.*

"It seems your shop is doing quite well; you could hire more help. If there's one thing I've learned in this life, time is short. Take time for the important things." Sadness washed over Grayson's face.

She ached to ease his pain. Her heart twisted. She covered his hand with hers.

five

Their eyes met.

Grayson's heart hammered.

Slowly, she moved her hand away from his and clasped both of hers in her lap, as if she feared they might betray her again. "I doubt very seriously that you ever neglected your wife."

He cleared his throat. "No, but I could've made more time. Now, it's too late to make up those precious hours."

"I'm sorry."

"At first, I was in shock and had to hold myself together for Dayne's sake. Then things calmed down and everyone else went on with their lives. For a while, it seemed the more time passed, the worse I missed her. Now, it depends on the day, the memories." He noticed tears building in her eyes. "I didn't mean to depress you."

"It's just very sad." She looked down at the table.

"It's actually nice to talk to someone." His fingers traced the intricate quilt line of the place mat. He struggled with the longing to reclaim the warmth of her hand. "Even after two years, people don't know what to say or fear the subject will upset me."

"They mean well."

"They do. I just wish everyone wouldn't treat me as if I might crack at the mere mention of Sara's name."

Grayson's cell vibrated and he jumped. "Excuse me." He stood to dig it from his pocket. "Hello?"

"Pastor Grayson?" Helen's voice quivered. "I'm sorry to interrupt your afternoon."

"Don't be. Tell me what's wrong."

"Wade's trying to check himself out of the treatment center."

"I'm glad you called. I'll be right over." He hung up.

"Let me get your coat." Adrea retrieved his suit jacket from the closet by the front door.

He slung the jacket over one shoulder and hurried out, sorry for Helen's distress, but relieved to have the excuse to get away from Adrea. Talking to her was simply too easy.

&

Three weddings and two funerals would keep the shop busy for the week. A wedding on Tuesday. Who would want to get married on a Tuesday?

Rachel worked tirelessly, right at Adrea's elbow. Normally, the sisters' affiliation worked well. While Adrea preferred immersing herself in flowers and rarely entered the glass-shelved, mirrored showroom, Rachel loved the customers and the sales end of the business. Though she often helped with arrangements, she found the solitude of the windowless work area stifling. Unless orders swamped them, she spent most of her time out front with the customers.

Yet this morning, Adrea couldn't shake Rachel. Each trip from the worktable to the floral refrigerator, Rachel tagged along. Initially, the subject had been Mark's sermon. However, Rachel soon got around to the topic of her interest.

"So, you seem to have spent some time with your new pastor." Rachel raised an eyebrow. "Haylee said something about a picnic in the park."

Casual. Keep it casual. "Haylee enjoyed it." She added more baby's breath to the bridesmaid bouquet. Maybe Rachel couldn't hear her heart beating double time.

"He's positively dreamy." Rachel packed the boutonnieres and corsages. "The stuff Christian romance novels are made of. I always thought the Prince Sterling nickname fit."

"If you like that type." From the corner of her eye, Adrea saw her sister taking in every expression and cracked under the pressure. "Okay, okay, he's really handsome and very nice. In fact, there should be a law against preachers being so easy on the eyes."

With a wistful expression, Rachel looked toward the ceiling. "I can just imagine him sweeping you into his arms."

"People don't get swept into each other's arms. They hug."

"Well, Curt and I never hug. He always sweeps me into his arms."

Adrea rolled her eyes. "Besides, Grayson Sterling is still mourning his wife."

"Maybe so. But you're alive." Rachel pointed an orange tiger lily at her.

"Just drop it. Please. For right now, he's my pastor. End of story." Adrea packed the cellophane bags containing boutonnieres and corsages into a cardboard box.

"Okay, if he's still in love with his wife, who has been gone for twoooo loooong yeeeears, why did he invite you on a picnic? And why did you take Haylee and Dayne with you?"

"It wasn't like that." Adrea propped her hands on her hips. "He didn't invite me. Haylee and I ran into him and Dayne at the park. It was totally unexpected, just like the first time I ran into him there."

"So, you seem to hang out in the park an awful lot lately."

"You know very well, the park is one of my favorite places." She scooted the full box across the tile floor with her foot with a *shwoosh*. "I jog three times a week, and it's where I go to unwind and relax."

"Maybe he's hanging out there in hopes of running into you."

Why is he there every time I turn around and never before? Maybe he's always been there and I just didn't know who he was. No, he's not the kind of man a woman overlooks.

"He has a young child. Kids like parks." *No way is he coming to the park in hopes of running into me.* "It's just coincidence. Besides, the church is bound to entangle our social lives. And on top of that, Mark is interested in his sister, Grace."

A big smile lit Rachel's eyes. "Well, Grayson Sterling has grieved long enough. He needs someone to make him happy again, and you are just the lady to do it."

"Rachel, please. He's still hurting. Let me take care of the romance in my life. Okay?"

"That's the problem. If left up to you, there is no romance in your life."

Adrea picked up a box. "I have to make deliveries."

"Nice escape."

Not really. She'd probably bump into Grayson, since the wedding was at Palisade.

Seven miles of highway passed as she dreaded running into the handsome pastor.

She turned into Palisade's parking lot, took several deep breaths, slowly exhaled, and got out of the van.

"I can help you."

She whirled around and almost dropped a large box.

Grayson—Pastor Grayson took the carton from her.

"Thanks." She was grateful for the extra muscle. Just wished they weren't his. A less attractive package would've been nice.

They made quick work of unloading. With everything inside the sanctuary, he hesitated.

"Need me to hold your ladder?"

"No thanks. I bought a new one."

He nodded and left her alone.

She added more bird-of-paradise to the archway. The orange spiky flowers with blue tongues gave it a funky look, per the bride's request. Adrea stood back to survey her handiwork. Not what she'd pick, but it held a certain charm. Satisfied, she rushed through the other decorations, willing the bride to hurry with her okay. Too late, the handsome pastor arrived.

"So, we'll be seeing one another often." He cleared his throat. "On a professional basis, of course."

"I guess so. Will someone be here in the morning, so I can pick up the arch and candelabrum?"

"Only my secretary. I'm going with Helen in the morning to the treatment center. But I can help you load up before I go."

"That's okay. It'll probably be later in the day before I come."

Just as soon as the bride made her final assessment and before she could change her mind, Adrea made a hasty escape.

At least she wouldn't run into him tomorrow.

❧

Mark's month-long trial had passed in a blur, and the congregation prepared to vote as he and Adrea left the church after Sunday morning services.

Offering what little comfort she could, Adrea took Mark's hand in hers. Pastor Grayson had promised to phone later with the results.

No matter how deeply the church would entrench Pastor Grayson in her life, Palisade would keep Mark close and in a short matter of months she'd gotten used to him being home.

Spring wildflowers carpeted the church lawn, pink primrose, scarlet Indian paintbrush, and the darkest violets, while birds chattered a welcome. Or was it good-bye?

"Guess what?" Mark clutched her hand tighter.

"What?"

"Grace agreed to have dinner with me. Alone."

"So, I don't have to go?"

"Not unless you want to double with Grayson."

She rolled her eyes.

After what seemed like an eternity, they made it to the car. Mark's hands shook as he started the engine.

"How about Dexter's?"

"It's a nice thought, but I couldn't eat a thing. Not even pizza."

"Me neither." She pressed a hand against the butterflies churning in her stomach.

"Let's go home. I don't know why I'm so nervous." Mark sighed.

"Just pray about it. God will work it out. Look at the bright side; even if they don't vote you in, you still got Grace out of the deal."

"I hadn't thought of it that way. Maybe that's why Grayson didn't want to make the decision himself. Maybe he knew from the beginning that Grace and I were clicking, and he didn't want the congregation to worry that I might get the position due to his or his sister's bias."

"Clicking, huh?"

Mark blushed, something Adrea had never seen him do before. For the first time, she realized that her brother didn't just have a crush. He was falling in love with Grace.

Back at the apartment, Mark and Adrea took turns pacing. She would have loved to go for a jog; however, she wanted to be at his side when Pastor Grayson called.

They both jumped when the phone rang.

"Get the cordless. I want you to hear the decision, too."

"Why?"

"So I won't have to repeat the conversation for you."

She retrieved the handset from a pile of magazines on the coffee table.

Mark practically pounced on the other phone.

Holding his free hand, she stood by his side.

He took a deep breath and pressed the receiver to his ear. "Hello?"

"The vote was unanimous, Mark. I hope and pray that you'll accept the position of associate pastor here at Palisade," Grayson said. "I'd like to meet with you tomorrow."

Adrea expelled the breath she hadn't realized she'd been holding.

"Okay, just give me a time." Mark wrote the details down and hung up.

Brother and sister hugged. Adrea's stomach growled and they both burst into giggles.

"I'm suddenly famished." She clutched her abdomen.

"Me, too."

"How about Dexter's?" they asked in unison.

❧

After much prayer, Mark accepted the position a few days later. Adrea embraced the decision as God's will, even though Mark's tenure cemented Grayson Sterling's place in their lives. She was proud of her brother, just out of seminary and now associate pastor at a church consisting of 150 people.

On Easter morning, Pastor Grayson announced, "I'm proud to add Brother Mark to our staff here at Palisade and pray that he'll stick around for years to come. He and his sister Adrea will be presented for membership after today's service."

The two men shook hands as the congregation clapped. The only member who seemed prouder than Mark and Adrea was Grace.

As they headed to Sunday school class, Grace stopped Adrea. "Grayson said you wanted to teach the children."

"Well, I. . ." She didn't want to tromp on Sara's memory. "I haven't been officially voted into membership yet."

Grayson stopped beside them. "You will be and Mrs. Jones is all set to help you with the transition." He seemed at peace. His tone even, no jaw twitching.

"If you're sure."

"I'll show you the way," Grace offered.

Adrea soon learned the kindergarten class included Dayne Sterling, since he would begin school in a few months. She adored the child. Though the little boy had his mother's fair coloring, except for those emerald eyes, his features and mannerisms reminded her of his father. A reminder she didn't need.

The children responded to her well and before she knew it, class ended.

"I don't think you need me hanging around. You're a natural." Mrs. Jones patted her arm.

"I've always loved kids." Her heart clenched. *Will I ever have any of my own?*

Back in the sanctuary, the lull between services was quiet. A few families dotted the pews, while most of the congregation lingered over coffee in the fellowship hall. Grace stood at the front, straightening the arrangement. Adrea joined her there.

The silk flowers, Easter and calla lilies with fern fronds and baby's breath looked old, frayed at the edge of each petal, as if someone had washed them too many times.

"I don't mean to overstep or take anyone's position, but if no one does the flowers, I'd love to."

Grace gasped, looking past Adrea.

She turned to see Grayson standing behind her.

"Sara always did the flowers." His voice was strained.

Adrea clasped a hand over her mouth, wishing she could melt through the floor. "I'm sorry. I—"

"No, it's okay." He frowned. "They're just flowers. We can't keep them forever."

"But—"

"They're getting undustable." He touched one of the white lilies.

Grace nodded. "I'll speak with Patty Deavers, the treasurer. She'll give you a check and go over what's in the flower budget."

⁂

The music began and the church started filling up. How many times could she trounce across Sara's grave in one day?

After services, Patty Deavers held a check toward Adrea. "Grace told me to give you this for flowers."

"Oh yes, of course." Adrea stuffed it into her wallet.

Patty scribbled a note and stashed it in her purse. "I'll get you a copy of the budget. In the meantime, I think Sara spent about a hundred per arrangement, so you'll be fine with that figure."

"Thanks, I'll put something together in the next few weeks."

"Adrea, how are you?"

She turned to see Helen. Wade's mother looked better. Fewer worry lines.

"Good. And you?"

"Wade's back in that horrible apartment in Searcy. I wanted him to go back to Missouri, away from that. . . He's working. So far, so good."

"We've been missing you at the shop." Adrea kissed a perfectly made-up cheek, trying not to think about Wade's blond floozy.

"And I've missed y'all, too. Since my time's freed up now, maybe I can get in a few days a week, like before."

"I've been wondering. . . Do the people here at church know about Wade and me?" *Namely, Grayson.*

"I don't really have close friends here that I talk about

Wade with. Pastor Grayson knows about the broken engagement, but I don't think I ever mentioned your name."

Sylvie Kroft shot a disdainful frown at Adrea.

"What did I do?" Adrea pressed a hand against her fluttery heart.

Helen sighed. "Nothing."

ॐ

Midweek, Adrea was still in her pajamas and doing her makeup when the doorbell chimed. With mascara applied to the lashes of her left eye, but not the right, she hurriedly slipped her robe on before checking the newly installed peephole.

Once she recognized their guest, she wished her brother could answer. Alas, Mark was in the shower. Grayson had caught Adrea in disarray entirely too many times. *What does it matter? There's no future for us.*

With no other choice, she answered the door.

Sadness clung to him like a shroud.

"What's wrong?"

"It's Helen. She fell and broke her hip."

"Oh no!" Adrea pressed a hand to her lips.

"I'm supposed to go by her house and pick up a few things she needs, but I don't know a thing about stuff like that. Grace is busy with a brunch of some kind, so I couldn't bother her with it."

"I'll take care of it. Want some coffee to go?"

Grayson sniffed the air. "Smells and sounds wonderful."

Mark sauntered into the room, already dressed.

"Helen broke her hip." Adrea poured a cup of coffee. "I'm going to pick up a few things for her."

"How is she?"

"In pain." Grayson sipped the hot brew. "The medication is helping."

"I've got two counseling sessions today." Mark checked his pocket calendar. "But I can stay with her tonight and relieve you."

"I'll probably take you up on it." Grayson headed for the door.

"I'll go get dressed." Adrea turned toward the hall.

"Um." Mark pointed to her eyes. "You might want to do something about that."

Her face burned. She'd forgotten all about her half-applied mascara.

An hour later, she arrived at the hospital and hurried up to Helen's room on the third floor. Doctors and nurses scurried about dressed in scrubs and smocks, their rubber-soled clogs squeaking on the polished tile floor.

Grayson sat beside Helen's bed.

"How good of you to come, Adrea." The older woman reached a trembly hand toward her young visitor.

Adrea clasped Helen's hand. "Of course I came. I had to see about my favorite lady. I'm so sorry. Are you in pain?"

"No, dear. Thank goodness Pastor Grayson came to check on me. I was hurting pretty badly and couldn't get to the phone. But they gave me something and now I'm just tired."

"We'll go and leave you alone so you can rest." Grayson stood.

"Please stay." Helen barely managed a whisper. "I love having you both here."

"I'll stay for a while if you stop talking and try to rest. How's that?" Adrea patted Helen's hand.

"Very well, I guess I do need a little nap." Her sad blue eyes closed and within minutes, her breathing evened and she began softly snoring.

Adrea gently withdrew her hand from Helen's limp grasp. Nodding at Pastor Grayson, she turned to go, but he followed.

"What did the doctor say?" she asked.

"It's a clean break and should heal well. They'll transfer her to their rehabilitation center when she's ready. It'll be a long, painful road, but he expects her to fully recover."

"Why did she fall? She's always been steady on her feet."

"She said she tried to get up too fast and got her foot caught in the sheet."

"Poor Helen." Adrea shook her head. "She's frailer than she

used to be—even more than just a few months ago. I cook for her sometimes, but I don't think she's eating well."

"Wade's problems have done a number on her."

On all of us.

☙

Saturday morning, Adrea hurried toward Helen's room.

"Adrea."

Heart pounding, she squeezed her eyes shut and turned around. Wade stood in the waiting room. She greeted him with a forced smile.

He looked like the man she used to know. The circles under his eyes had receded. Groomed hair, neat clothing, sober.

"How's Helen?"

"Comfortable. Mark was here when I arrived."

Great. "How'd that go?"

"Civil. I'm sorry about the way I've acted lately."

"I'm just glad you're doing better."

"Much better. I got reacquainted with God and I'm back in church."

Just what she'd prayed for. "I'm glad. Really glad."

"I could still use your prayers. Shell ditched me in Missouri, and I followed her back here." Raw pain shone in his eyes. "She's pregnant. I'm trying to patch things up with her, but so far, she's not interested."

Despite the reminder of the children they'd planned together, his despair tugged at her. She touched his shoulder.

She caught movement out of the corner of her eye. Grayson entered the waiting room.

Wade's jaw twitched.

Her hand dropped to her side.

A frown furrowed Grayson's brow.

Confusion with a tad of disappointment.

He cleared his throat. "Is Helen awake?"

☙

Grayson, along with Mark, Adrea, and Grace did their best to keep Helen company since her move to rehab. Several members from Palisade visited, as well. Grayson often ran into Adrea there and a few times, they shared coffee.

In the cafeteria, Grayson chose a table near the door, so he could watch for her, as always, looking forward to the extra chance to see her. He drummed his fingers on the melamine table, hoping she'd show before he had to leave.

The scene with Wade and Adrea had played through his mind several times in the last month. Sober so far, Wade had a new job in Searcy. An alcoholic working at a country club? Par for the course of a golf instructor.

Grayson took a swig of the lukewarm, knock-the-top-of-your-head-off coffee.

Hopefully, whatever was between Wade and Adrea was over. Was that selfish? Wade needed her. With Adrea in his life, he might have incentive to stay sober. But she certainly didn't need Wade.

Adrea stepped off the elevator. A breath of late-spring air dressed in a pale green top and white short pants. *What do they call those things? Capris?* Whatever they were, they showed off her slender ankles.

His heart skipped a beat.

"Would you like some bad coffee?" *Great line.*

"I'll just go see Helen first."

"The nurse ran me out."

"All right then." She hesitated at his table, then got her cup and added two creams and two sugars, just like she always did. With no further way to delay, she took the seat across from him.

"Helen's making an amazing recovery."

Distracted by something, Adrea didn't respond.

He followed her gaze.

Sylvie Kroft headed their way.

She stopped at their table, apparently speechless, a rare occurrence for her. Grayson could see the wheels of gossip spinning.

"Well, well." She found her tongue. "Isn't this cozy."

"Hello, Sylvie." *Calm and casual. Nothing of interest going on here.* "We're just celebrating Helen's speedy recuperation. Her therapist plans to release her next week. Isn't that wonderful?"

"Just grand. Did the two of you come here together?"

"No, I had no idea Pastor Grayson was here." Adrea traced the rim of her Styrofoam cup. "We just ran into each other."

"What a coincidence. Why just last week, Mrs. Jones said how nice it was that you two had visited Mrs. Fenwick."

Poor Adrea. Her usually smiling mouth pulled into a tight line. With jerky movements, she set her cup down, sloshing steaming liquid on the table. She shouldn't have to defend the completely innocent situation. Well, maybe not completely innocent.

He often caught himself not thinking of Helen's injury at all, but instead, his mind strayed to the lovely woman sitting across from him. Curbing his thoughts, fearing Sylvie might somehow read them, Grayson took a sip of his tepid coffee.

"We've both been checking on her often. We don't want her to feel lonely."

"That's nice." Sylvie smirked. "She doesn't have anyone except that horrible Wade."

"Several people from church have visited with her since she's been here. I'm really glad we have such a supportive church family." Grayson frowned for effect. "We haven't seen you here before or at the hospital. Is this your first visit, or have we just missed each other?"

Sylvie's coral-tinted lips moved like a gasping fish out of water, then twisted into a fake smile. "Well, I've been busy. I'll leave you two alone to visit or. . .whatever it was you were doing. I'll just go see Mrs. Fenwick now."

"You do that." Grayson smiled.

She glanced back over her shoulder several times until she disappeared through double doors. Sylvie's husband, an alcoholic, never stepped foot in church. Their two children, both grown and gone with lives of their own, never came for a visit. Instead of having empathy for the plight of Helen and Wade, since alcoholism controlled Sylvie's life as well, she took all her heartache and picked apart the lives of others.

Grayson prayed for her daily.

Adrea sipped her coffee. "Why does she hate me?"

"It's not you. Sylvie's life isn't. . .easy. She lives next door to Sara's parents, over in Searcy, and I think she got the impression they were the perfect family. Her daughter was friends with Grace and Sara. Sylvie idolized Sara."

"I hope she won't bother Helen about Wade." Adrea downed the last of her coffee. "Maybe she'll have enough gossip concerning us."

"What can she say?" Grayson asked. "We're sitting in an extremely public place having coffee."

"She'll say something. I'm certain of it." She stood and threw her coffee cup away. "I need to get back to the shop, so I'll check on Helen and be on my way."

Grayson watched her go with a hitch in his heart. He always hated it when she left.

He'd been praying about his developing feelings for her, and somehow he got the impression Sara approved. Adrea loved Jesus and the church. She loved kids. She was great with Dayne, older people, and the hospitalized.

What if I let myself fall for her and she dies? Just like Sara.

No. Better to stifle such wandering feelings. He had enough people to worry about.

❧

After class, Adrea returned to the sanctuary through the side door. A hush settled over the crowd already there. She'd noticed it all morning. Sylvie had done her job.

Helen was sitting in her usual spot. Her first Sunday back. Though she walked stiffly, with a walker, she'd even made it for class.

Whispers swished through the assembly, with several members looking toward the back of the sanctuary. Adrea glanced over her shoulder. Her jaw dropped.

six

Despite the long hair hanging in his eyes, Adrea recognized the man flanked by Jack and Grayson. Wade stumbled down the aisle of Palisade.

Mark hurried toward her. "What's he doing here?"

When Wade tripped, Grayson steadied him.

Wade jerked his arm away. "I can walk on my own."

"I'll sit with you." Mark put a protective arm around her shoulders.

"No, you go on up front. I'll be fine. He's so far gone he may not even recognize me."

"Wishful thinking on your part."

Mark claimed his usual seat beside Grace and Dayne. Adrea hurried to the back of the sanctuary.

Wade sat beside Helen, tears rolling down her cheeks. She didn't need this.

Despite his rough appearance, the congregation welcomed him. Several greeted him and Adrea heard snippets of how much his mother meant to them. With each greeting, Wade seemed more miserable.

Sylvie Kroft kept her distance, but her eyes never left his disheveled appearance.

The well-trained pastor's son ran to meet the visitor and offered his hand. "I'm Dayne Sterling. Nice to have you at Palisade."

Wade started crying.

Adrea's heart lurched.

Grace hurried to retrieve her confused nephew.

Knowing Helen needed support, Adrea waited until the harpist began then forced herself to move forward and claim her usual seat on the other side of Helen. The whiff of alcohol turned her stomach. Wade was so out of it, he

80

didn't notice her presence at first. By the time he did, the congregational hymns had already begun.

During the song service, he jiggled his feet and twiddled his thumbs. Adrea watched him from under her lashes. His palpable nervousness proved contagious. She half expected him to break and run.

Grayson launched into his sermon. "People think they have to clean up before they come to Christ. They think they have to beat their demons before He will accept them. The complete opposite is true. If you'll just trust Him, He'll clean you up. He'll take your burdens away. Jesus Christ will instill in your heart the desire to come clean. Commit yourself to Jesus and He'll wash all your sins away."

Halfway through the message, Wade had the entire pew bouncing as he trembled.

To drive his point home, Grayson quoted 2 Corinthians 5:17. "Therefore if any man be in Christ, he is a new creature: old things are passed away; behold, all things are become new."

The hymn began as everyone bowed their heads. Adrea felt certain at least half the church prayed for the jittering man seated beside his mother. The second verse began and Wade squirmed even more. Several people knelt at the altar.

Adrea continued to pray. Finally, as if he could stand it no longer, just as the song neared its conclusion, he sprang to his feet and staggered toward the altar.

Helen stood and made slow progress with her walker. Two deacons rushed to Wade's side. As his stance tilted precariously, the men steadied him.

Pastor Grayson stepped off the stage and whispered something to Mark, then went to meet Wade. The entire congregation seemed to hold its collective breath.

Finally, Wade made it to the front and knelt at the intricate, hand-carved altar, joined by Grayson and eventually Helen. The song leader started the hymn over and after all four verses, ended again. Wade kept sobbing.

Mark stood. "Pastor Grayson would like the deacons to stay. Tom Deavers will offer the closing prayer and everyone else is dismissed afterward."

After Tom's prayer, the congregation filtered out of the pews and moved to the back of the church. Sylvie Kroft sat rooted to her seat, until Grace offered to walk her out.

In the lobby, Grace stopped beside Adrea. "Since Mark's tied up, Dayne and I can take you home."

"Thanks, but I think I'll wait for Mark." Her heart hammered in her ears.

"It might be awhile and Grayson can take him home. I learned a long time ago, never to ride with my brother. That way I don't get stranded here."

"I'll be fine. I want to make sure Helen's okay anyway."

"What was wrong with that man?" Dayne asked.

"He's real sick, sweetie." Grace patted her nephew's shoulder. "But he came to the right place."

Adrea waved as they left then went to her car and tried to enjoy the peaceful late May weather.

The parking lot cleared, leaving only a handful of vehicles behind. A few minutes later, the church door opened and Grayson ran to his car, followed by Mark and Tom.

Adrea frowned. What was going on?

None of the men seemed to notice her as they passed, with Mark driving.

Adrea didn't know what to do. Go home or wait and see if Mark came back. As she tried to decide, the church door burst open. Wade stumbled out and headed straight for Helen's sedan. Tires screeched as he tore out of the parking lot.

She watched until he was out of sight, praying that no one ended up in his path. Then Helen came out of the church and Adrea ran to meet her.

"Where did he go?" Tears streamed down the older woman's face.

"I don't know, but he took your car."

"Go after him. Please." The urgency in Helen's eyes convinced Adrea to do as asked.

"How will you get home?"

"A deacon will take care of me. Just please go to his apartment. Make sure he arrives safely."

❧

Adrea climbed the rusty stairs to Wade's room.

With no response to her hesitant knock, she tried the knob. Greasy, but unlocked. Dreading the encounter, she pushed the door open.

He sat on the sagging couch. The refuse around him wasn't as bad as last time, but getting there. A glass of clabbered milk made her gag. She trekked through the strewn-about trash to take the putrid liquid to the kitchen sink, just to get it out of smelling distance. She shivered.

"Wade? Are you all right?"

"What are you doing here?"

"You tell me. Helen asked me to come."

"How is Mom?" His chin quivered.

"She was upset." Adrea perched on the well-worn sofa arm.

"I'm. . .leaving later." He touched her hair and traced her jaw with his fingertips.

She turned away. "Don't."

"If only I'd loved you the way you deserved to be loved, we'd have gotten married and none of this would've happened."

Unwilling to take the trip down memory lane, she studied her chipped, jagged fingernails, fighting the urge to nibble. "So, what happened at the church?"

He ran his hand through his hair and patted the seat next to him. "Come sit beside me. I won't try anything. I promise."

As she scooted over next to him, he fished a flask out of his jacket and tipped it to his lips.

She stood. "I won't stay if you drink."

"Sorry, I just really need it." He put it away.

"No you don't." She reclaimed her seat. Matted cotton protruded from a rip that ran the entire length of the armrest and a spring lodged in her back. "So, you've been drinking and you drove your mother's car. Do you realize how dangerous that is?"

He snickered. "Trust me, I'm well aware of the dangers, but

I had to get out of there."

"What's going on with you?"

"I should have owned up to this a long time ago. There's not much time. The cops will get here soon."

"Why?" Her mind raced. What had Wade done?

"What should have been our wedding day was the beginning of the end."

She remembered the date with a shudder.

"I took a little trip to Jacksonville."

The nearest liquor store. "Oh, Wade."

"It gets worse. Much worse. After I left the liquor store, I went to a bar in Little Rock. I guess I'd parked illegally or something because when I got ready to leave, my car was gone." The more he talked, the faster the long pent-up words tumbled out. "I walked probably a mile, but I was tired, so I stopped at a hotel. I found a car with the keys in it."

"You stole a car?" She tucked one leg under the other and turned to face him.

"I was just planning to borrow it. I would have brought it back the next day, I swear."

"Couldn't you have gotten a cab?"

"I wish I had." He covered his face with both hands. His shoulders quaked.

Hesitantly, she touched his back and he pulled her into his arms. His sobs shook them both.

"What happened?"

"I hit another car in El Paso."

"You what?" A glimpse of Sara Sterling's image in the newspaper flitted through Adrea's mind. It couldn't be. "Did you stop? Did you call the police?"

"No."

She pulled away from him and jumped up. "You hit another car and you just kept going!"

"I hoped it was a nightmare. That I'd only hit a Dumpster or something." Wade stood and paced away from her.

"But it wasn't. It was a car. With an innocent family inside."

He whirled toward her, guilt etched into his features. "I

was scared. I didn't want to go to jail, so I abandoned the car and hitchhiked home. Next morning, I got mine out of the impound lot and headed to my aunt's in Missouri. Shell followed me and we got a place. Been drinking pretty much ever since. Every time I think about it, I see that woman with the car crumpled around her."

"Sara Sterling." Adrea began pacing now. Tears fell as realization set in. *He was drinking because of me. It's my fault she's dead.*

He noticed her reaction. "Did you know her?"

"No. But, I've done her flowers for years." White roses at the cemetery. *Because of me.*

"It's been eating me alive." Wade buried his face in his hands again. "Then who showed up at my door a few months ago and dragged me off to rehab? Like some nightmare. Then to top it off, he and that deacon hauled me to church this morning and there was that kid. Welcomed me, shook my hand, like a miniature little preacher or something. And all I could think was, 'I killed your mama.'"

"You have to turn yourself in."

He didn't answer, just paced some more. The scuffed wooden floor creaked with each step.

"Wade? You plan to call the police, don't you?"

"Sure." He didn't sound convincing. "But somebody at the church probably already called. I made a full confession."

She walked over beside him and touched his forearm. "I'll go with you to the station."

"No, you go home. I'll wait here for them. I killed that woman on my own. I need to do this on my own."

His words made her more confident that he would do the right thing. "Does Shell know?"

He winced. "We were patching things up. I wanted to start fresh, so I told her. She split and killed my kid without even consulting me." Tears dripped from his chin.

A knife sliced through her heart for the innocent baby. No words came.

"Did you hear me?"

"I'm sorry. Truly, I am. Does your mom know about the baby?"

"I was hoping to tell her after Shell married me. Now, it's too late." His chin trembled. "I told Mom about the accident at the church. Take care of her for me. She'll need you to get her through this."

"I will." Despite the gravity of his confession and all the pain he'd caused, she felt sorry for him. She hugged him, but he pulled away.

"You better go."

"Let's pray."

"Me and Jesus got it all worked out."

"That's good to know."

"Go," he said. "You don't need to be mixed up in this any more than you already are."

"I'm sorry, Wade."

He cupped her face in his hands. "None of this is your fault. It was all me. I started drinking because of our breakup, but I gave you good reason to call off the wedding."

Adrea gave him one more quick hug. "I'm proud of you for coming clean."

With a tender kiss on her cheek, he ushered her out.

In a haze, she descended the stairs.

Wade killed Sara Sterling. *Because of me.* Now after two years, he confessed. *I can't let him do this alone.*

She turned to go back up the steps. *Boom!* The blast almost sent her reeling. She fell backward but managed to grab the railing and right herself. A knot formed in her stomach.

Two at a time, she ran up the rest of the stairs. Curious, other tenants came out of their rooms. Adrea bypassed them. The door was slightly ajar. With absolute dread coursing through her entire body, she pushed it open. Wade lay on the couch.

The scene didn't really register in her dazed consciousness. There was something horribly wrong with his head. Hands trembling, she dialed 911.

Wade was dead.

2&

But he wasn't. When the police arrived, they barely detected Wade's pulse. Soon paramedics pushed through the crowd. Adrea couldn't watch. Forcing her way through the spectators huddled just outside the open apartment door, she made her way to the steps and sat.

"Oh, Lord, please help." Unable to utter a sensible prayer, she rocked back and forth.

More curious bystanders made their way up to the second level, stepping around her.

She stood and turned sideways.

Finally, the paramedics carried Wade out on a gurney.

Her gut wrenched. He was still, his skin a sickening shade of gray, his head swathed in bandages.

"I'm his friend. Is he alive?"

"Barely."

"Are you taking him to the local hospital?"

"We're MedFlighting him to Little Rock."

Helen. With clumsy fingers, she dialed Mark's cell phone.

"Where are you?" Mark asked.

"He shot himself."

"Who?"

"Wade shot himself. He's alive, but barely. They're taking him to Little Rock."

"Meet me at Helen's and I'll take y'all there."

"How is Grayson?"

"A mess."

Adrea hung up and dashed down the stairs to her car.

"Adrea!"

She turned to see Birney Wilson, dressed in his Searcy police uniform, heading in her direction. Since she usually only saw him at Mountain Grove, it jarred her to see him in his professional role.

"You okay?"

"Not really." She leaned on the railing.

"Someone said you were with him?"

"Not when he. . .did it. Just before."

"You know you'll have to come to the station."

"Why?"

"You were the last person to see him. . .before." He scribbled something on a small notebook.

"Am I a suspect?" A hard knot formed in the pit of her stomach. "He shot himself."

"We haven't ruled on that yet."

"But, I wasn't there. I was leaving."

"Yes, several witnesses said they saw you leaving before the shot. Don't worry, Adrea. It's standard procedure with this kind of case to question everyone in the area."

"Helen needs me."

"It won't take long." He rested his hand on her shoulder. "Ride with me. You're too shaky to drive."

She nodded and followed him to a squad car. On the way, she called Mark again.

№

A tattooed suspect shuffled past in shackles. Adrea stared at the floor.

A man's legs stopped in front of her.

"Adrea?"

She launched into her brother's arms. "Oh, Mark, it was so horrible."

"I know, sweetheart." He stroked her hair. "I'm so sorry you were there."

"I can't believe he killed Sara." Her chin trembled. "How is Helen?"

"She's on her way to the hospital. Jack, Tom, and their wives are with her."

"What about Grayson?"

"I took him home. Grace is there."

"How is he?"

"Still a mess." Mark raked his fingers through his hair. "They both are."

"What about Dayne?"

"His grandfather came and picked him up. Stop worrying about everyone else. Tell me why you're here."

"She was a witness." Birney motioned them to his office. Closing the door, he gestured toward two metal chairs facing him. He handed her a cup of coffee and took a seat behind his charcoal metal desk.

Too strong and black. She didn't care. Maybe it would calm the butterflies flopping in her stomach. She took a big gulp and scalded her tongue.

"Do you mind if I record our conversation?" Birney set a recorder on the desk.

"Of course not."

Birney clicked a button. "So tell me, why were you with Wade?"

"He showed up at church. Drunk. After the service, Wade went to the altar. He left upset and his mother asked me to follow him."

Mark leaned forward. "Has there been anything new in the case of Sara Sterling? Any new leads?"

Adrea set the coffee cup down with a clatter and looked out the window at Birney's view, a brick wall.

"I'm not at liberty to discuss that information." Birney steepled his fingers.

"Wade claimed he was the hit-and-run driver." Mark put his arm around Adrea. "He confessed at the church. There were several witnesses, including Grayson Sterling."

"I see." Birney digested the news for a moment.

"He confessed to me, too." Adrea gulped a deep breath. "Right before. . ."

Mark took her hand. "Can her name be kept out of the papers?"

"You have my word." Birney ran his palm along the back of his neck. "Now, let's get into exactly what Wade confessed to."

☙

Mark found a space in the hospital parking lot and killed the engine. "I shouldn't have brought you here."

Adrea stared out the window. Several iron benches surrounded a fountain in front of the entrance. "Did Wade tell everyone at church why he was drinking that night?"

"He never needed a reason, did he?"

"It should have been our wedding day."

"So now you plan on blaming yourself?"

"It's my fault." Her words ended on a sob.

Mark pulled her into his arms. "No, Adrea. You can't think that way. Think about why you broke up with him. It wasn't on a whim. And you didn't put the bottle in his hands or make him steal that car."

"No, but I might as well have. Sara Sterling is dead. Because of me."

He gave her a gentle shake. "Don't ever say that again. Don't even think it. Sara Sterling is dead because Wade Fenwick is a loser who blames his problems on everyone else and drowns them in alcohol instead of facing up to his own failures. If you had married him, and thank God you didn't, he probably would have drank to get through the ceremony. You are not responsible for Wade's drinking or Sara's death. Do you hear me?"

She nodded.

On the fourth floor, two deacons and their wives waited with Helen, but no Grayson.

Adrea steeled herself and stepped into the ICU waiting room. A family huddled together, communicating with sniffles and hugs.

"Oh, Adrea, how good of you to come." Even under extreme duress, Helen had manners. "I just can't believe it."

"Me, neither." Adrea sat beside the older woman.

"He's still in surgery. I should have known." Helen wrung her hands. "Wade went to my sister June's on February 15th. Couldn't get out of here fast enough. I remember being so upset about Sara, but I never imagined the two were connected. I thought he just wanted to make a new start."

"I'm so sorry." Adrea put her arm around Helen's trembling shoulders.

"I'll never be able to face Pastor Grayson again. Or Sylvie Kroft. I'll have to find a new church. Maybe, I'll move away. To June's."

"No, Helen. He wouldn't want you to do that. No one at Palisade would. Everyone loves you and right now, you need your church family. Don't even think about Sylvie. This is your home."

Helen straightened her posture. "Mark, I want you to take Adrea home and go check on Pastor Grayson."

Mark shook his head. "We're not leaving you alone."

"I'm not alone and June's on her way. She's barely over the Missouri line, so it won't be but a few hours before she arrives."

"We'll stay until she gets here." Adrea patted her hand.

&

Adrea wasn't the least bit tired, despite the roller-coaster day. "Drop me here and check on Grayson."

Mark parked in front of their apartment. "That was my plan. You sure you'll be okay?"

With the balcony windows open, her garden beckoned. "I'm fine. Is that Rachel's car?"

"I called her while you were with Helen."

"Does she know what's happened?"

"I filled her in." He kissed her cheek. "I didn't want you to be alone."

She checked her watch. "We missed church?" She couldn't remember the last time.

"Tom Deavers got a fill-in to handle it."

Once inside, Rachel greeted her with a hug.

Adrea went out to sit in the garden and her sister took the cue. Not in the mood to talk. For the first time, the abundant flowers didn't soothe her soul. She cupped a cool yellow rose with jittery fingers, wondering how Grayson was doing.

She went back inside to pace the small living room.

Rachel sat in the kitchen, her elbows propped on the table. "Why don't you take a shower and go to bed."

"I won't be able to sleep, but a shower might relax me."

It didn't work. As the evening wore on, her shoulders ached with tension. In the middle of blow-drying her hair, the doorbell sounded.

When she stepped into the living room, Grayson stood

there, shoulders slumped, his face the picture of anguish.

"Sit down." She gestured to the sofa. Realizing what she wore, a blush heated her cheeks. Though the leopard-spot pajama shirt and pants were perfectly decent, not exactly the appropriate attire for greeting one's pastor. "I'll be right back."

"I'll make coffee." Rachel filled the pot.

"Just give me a minute." Adrea hurried to the bedroom to put on her jeans and T-shirt but caught a glimpse of herself in the mirror. Scrubbed free of makeup, her face was pale and splotchy. Her half-dried hair stuck out at odd angles. She brushed it into place and headed back to the living room. The best she could do. Besides, he'd barely looked at her.

"I'll be in your room." Rachel hurried down the hall.

Grayson waited until they were alone. "Sorry to bother you. I'm kind of thrown for a loop and not even sure why I came here. I guess I wanted to talk to somebody somewhat removed from the situation."

Removed. *I caused the whole thing.* "Mark just went to check on you."

"Maybe he can help Grace. I'm not much good to anyone right now."

"I'm sure everyone understands."

The coffeemaker gurgled and spewed as the rich aroma filled the kitchen.

"For over two years, I've dreamt of finding Sara's killer. Dreamt of smashing the guy's face in and breaking his legs with my bare hands. Not very pastoral thoughts."

"You're only human."

"I never imagined it might be someone I know."

Me neither. "I'm sure that makes it even harder." Her voice cracked.

"Today, I dragged him to church, with no idea *who* he was. I guess all these run-ins with me spurred his confession."

"Makes sense." That and meeting Dayne.

He covered his face with both hands. His shoulders shook.

Adrea didn't know what to do. She moved to the chair beside him and tentatively touched his arm.

Covering her hand with one of his, he made an effort to pull himself together. She handed him a tissue and he mopped his face.

Grabbing two mugs from the counter, she poured coffee in each, then set the creamer and sugar on the table. "How do you take yours?"

"Just black tonight." Steam swirled from his cup as he tipped it to his lips. "Since Sara died, I've had—the doctor calls them panic attacks. Like in the park that day. Shortness of breath, tightness in my chest, headaches. The first time, I thought it was my heart. Anything sets them off. A passing ambulance, not knowing where Dayne is or Grace. Even my parents."

"That's understandable. Considering what you've been through." So scarred by the loss of his wife, the sight of their child running toward the street, brought on near hyperventilation. *And it's my fault.*

He took another sip of coffee. "I know it's irrational, but with the driver off the streets, for the first time, I feel we're safe. Isn't that crazy? I mean, just because one drunk driver tries to blow himself away, it doesn't mean there aren't a million others out there."

The image of Wade putting the gun to his head chilled her soul.

"The doctor said if he survives, he'll be a vegetable. I'm glad he won't be able to hurt anyone else. I know I shouldn't think that way, but I can't help it."

Part of her agreed with him. The other part still grieved the man she'd once loved. A weight settled across her shoulders.

A key clicked in the lock and Mark stepped inside. "There you are, Grayson. I just left Grace. Your folks are there. They're all worried sick about you."

"What about Dayne?"

"Asleep. He doesn't know what's happened. They figure it's your call."

"I went to tell Sara's parents."

Mark winced. "Bet that was tough."

"I can't get Helen off my mind. I should be with her."

"She's worried about you. Her sister made it in and Wade survived surgery. He's stable." He glanced at Adrea. "June talked Helen into going home until morning."

"I'll call Grace, so she won't worry." Adrea headed to her room. "I should have done that already, but I'm not thinking very clearly."

"Adrea," Grayson called.

She turned to face him.

"Thanks."

She nodded then left the men alone.

Rachel sat on her bed, cell phone in hand. "Here she is. I'll call you later."

"Go on home, Rachel."

"That was Mom. They just got out of church. They want to be sure you're okay."

"I'm fine." Grabbing a yellow satin and lace throw pillow, she hugged it to her stomach and plopped down beside her sister.

"Did Grayson leave?" Rachel put an arm around her shoulders.

"No. Mark's home. I left so they could talk."

"What a mess. I never dreamed it would be Wade."

"Me neither." Adrea laid her head on Rachel's shoulder.

❧

Parked in the hospital lot in Little Rock, Grayson sat with Sara's white Bible clutched against his chest. He turned to the familiar indentation between two worn pages. The white rose Sara had insisted on taking to dinner that night, forever preserved. The white rose Sara had died holding, placed to mark her favorite Bible verse. With tear-blurred vision, he couldn't read it. He knew it by heart. Isaiah 41:10.

"Fear thou not; for I am with thee: be not dismayed; for I am thy God: I will strengthen thee; yea, I will help thee; yea, I will uphold thee with the right hand of my righteousness."

He longed for peace beyond all understanding, but it didn't come. He cupped the white rose in the palm of his hand, careful not to damage the dry crispness.

How he'd delighted in her joy at each arrangement. Other women would probably take the roses for granted. But on each occasion, Sara's pale blue eyes sparkled; she'd trace his jaw with her fingers, and reward him with a kiss.

Pressing his fingertips to his lips, desperate to recall the feel of her that last day, his chest tightened.

He slammed his fist into the dash.

A car door shut beside him. His deacon, Tom Deavers, waved, sympathy shining, then headed in Grayson's direction.

Grayson waved back with a forced smile. He was sick of sympathy. He didn't want sympathy. He wanted his wife. He wanted to smash his fist into the face of Wade Fenwick, who'd stolen Sara from him. Too spineless to come forward. Until now. *Just when I've begun to heal.*

Gripping the steering wheel, white knuckled, he forced himself to step out of the vehicle. "I was hoping you'd still be on duty. Can I see Wade Fenwick?"

"Visiting hours ended at eight o'clock." Tom looked suspicious.

"I'm not here to cause any trouble."

Tom's eyes narrowed. "Follow me."

Inside, they took the stairs, then corridor after corridor, to ICU. Grayson had sat with numerous families in this very waiting area.

"You can go in, for a few minutes."

"Thank you."

Grayson hurried down the hall.

No family, no medical personnel. Wade was alone with a machine helping him breathe. His chest inflated and deflated, with a jerky, mechanical *whoosh*. The overwhelming desire to ram his fist into the helpless man's swollen face gripped Grayson. Visions of movies where the bad guy unplugged the ventilator played in his imagination. His fingers flexed as he surveyed all the tubes and wires.

Sobbing, Grayson sank to his knees. "Dear Lord, he killed Sara. He ruined my life. He ruined my son's life. Oh God, help me. Forgive me. Help me to forgive."

seven

Just as Adrea finished dressing the next morning, she heard a knock and hurried to answer.

Grace leaned against the door frame, tears flowing down her cheeks.

"Oh, honey, I'm so sorry." Adrea hugged her and drew her inside.

"I'll get you something to drink," Mark said.

Grace pulled away from Adrea and flew into his arms.

Adrea quietly exited the apartment.

With a few moments to spare, she drove by the church. As usual, Grayson's car was there. The upheaval in his life didn't change his calling.

She made her way to the office and found him, slumped over his desk, facedown. For a moment, she thought he was asleep, but he raised up.

"I thought I heard someone. Sit. What can I do for you?"

With his world blown apart, still he wanted to help others.

"Can't stay long." She claimed the chair across from him. "I'm on my way to the shop. Listen, I know you've got a lot going on and I can't imagine how you're holding it together."

"I'll be fine."

"You've been dealt quite a blow. But, Helen needs you. Last night, she was worrying about being able to face you. She mentioned changing churches or maybe moving to her sister's."

Grayson looked heavenward. "I got here at five o'clock this morning and have been praying for strength to go over there. I think I've steeled myself."

"You don't have to be strong for her. Maybe the two of you need to cry together."

He nodded.

Other than telling Dayne that Sara was dead and going to the funeral, this was the hardest thing Grayson had ever done. Helen was probably blaming herself and he wanted to be strong for her, but right now, he didn't have a strong bone in his body.

In Helen's drive, he sat for a long time. The flower beds and grass weren't perfect as they'd once been. Green vines grew wild, jumping their borders. Dead plants jutted among the blooming bushes. Maybe someone from the youth group could help with her yard.

The kitchen light flicked on. With a quick prayer, he got out and walked to the door. Before he could knock, she answered. He'd never seen such anguish in another person's eyes. The sobs started and her whole body shook. Afraid she might collapse; he picked her up and carried her inside.

"I've got you, and God has both of us. His strength will get us through this. Together."

"I can't believe this is happening. Wade caused Sara's death." A wail escaped and she pressed a trembling fist to her mouth.

He deposited her on the couch and settled beside her.

"Our precious Sara killed by a drunk driver. And not just any drunk driver. My son."

Grayson didn't know how to respond. He took her shaking hand in his. "Dear God, get us through this."

An hour later, he drove Helen and June to the hospital. Upon their arrival, Mark and Grace sat in the waiting room. As the afternoon lengthened, various members of the congregation trickled in. The deacons and Sylvie Kroft, of course.

It almost felt like Sara had died all over again. People patted his shoulder, offering comforting whispers.

Helen sat ramrod straight, not a crinkle in her composure. How did she do it?

"Mrs. Fenwick." The doctor's face was grim. "I need to speak with you."

Grayson didn't think his legs would support him, but he managed to stand and help Helen to her feet. They followed the doctor down the hallway.

Saturday afternoon, Adrea exited the hospital with Helen's hand tucked in her elbow. Grayson, made of steel, carried her suitcase to the car.

Wade would move into a regular room in a few days, though he would never talk, walk, or function on his own. Even in a wheelchair, someone else would have to prop him there.

Once outside in the bright sunshine, Helen paused at the bench by the fountain.

The trickling water soothed Adrea's frayed nerves. "Would you like to sit down?"

"It's been a week since I've seen the sun." Helen gingerly perched on the bench. "I feel guilty. Wade will never enjoy the sun again."

"You have to go on."

"I know." Helen's watery blue eyes brimmed. "I've done it before. With my husband and my youngest sister. For some reason, I seem destined to end up alone."

Adrea sat and put her arm around Helen's slim shoulders. "You're not alone. You've got Jesus and a church full of people who love you."

"Shell's only been to see Wade once."

Yesterday, Adrea had seen the blond girl at the hospital and had banished the memories that threatened to stir. "She's hurting, too."

Helen's piercing blue eyes searched Adrea's soul.

The moment of reckoning. She'd dreaded it for days.

"He was drinking on the night of the accident because of me."

Helen clasped her hand. "No. We had him so late in life, and I spoiled him so badly, he never learned to handle disappointment. Wade was drinking because that's what he did."

"But, he'd been sober for two years. He started again because of our breakup."

"He gave you ample reason to call off the wedding. I love that boy, but I know exactly what he put you through and you didn't deserve any of it."

"Neither did you."

The older woman scanned the azure horizon. "He told me he was going to turn himself in." A sob caught in her throat. "Instead—this."

"I'm so sorry. I should have seen it coming."

"You tried to help him. He should have come forward when it happened."

Instead, he'd waited until everyone had made tentative steps to get on with their lives. Then he'd blown all efforts apart. Grayson knew the identity of the hit-and-run driver, and the knowledge forced him to relive Sara's death all over again. Poor Helen. Even in a vegetative state, Wade was breaking his mother's heart.

Adrea's hands clenched. She could almost hate him, until she thought of his torment when he'd confessed.

"After he told me about what happened, I asked if he wanted to pray. He said, 'Me and Jesus got it all worked out.'"

Helen closed her eyes. A trembling smile tilted the corners of her mouth. "Thank you for being there for him."

❧

Monday morning, Adrea stashed her purse under the counter in the workroom.

"There's some redhead tormenting the salesclerks." Rachel propped both hands on her hips. "Said she knows you from church."

"Sylvie Kroft?" *Surely not. She's never bothered to darken our door before.*

"That's her." Rachel snapped her fingers. "I better go see if I can hurry her along before they lose all patience."

Adrea checked the computer for standing orders.

June 2nd, what should have been Sara's twenty-seventh birthday. Had it only been a few months since Wade had dropped the Valentine's Day roses? Now, he lay in a hospital bed. Sara's killer. Wade would never hold another beer can, never drive a car, and never hurt anyone else. She knew the news comforted Grayson, while he comforted Wade's distraught mother.

Nothing made sense. She felt like she was watching some

surreal movie. The man she'd almost married, a shell of himself, all he'd ever be.

She began working with the white flowers, the rose of innocence and reverence, and shed a few tears as she always did. As the arrangement took shape, she thought of Grayson, as usual, and his motherless son. No child should have to take roses to his mother at the cemetery.

Adding more caspia, she turned the arrangement slowly around, looking for any other holes to fill. Would Grayson even remember the roses? Of course he would. He'd comfort Helen, take care of Dayne, and stroll in later. As if nothing were wrong, he'd personally sign the card and deliver the roses to the cemetery. Where Sara shouldn't be.

The showroom door opened, interrupting her thoughts.

"I'm afraid the roses aren't quite ready, Pastor Grayson." Rachel backed into the workroom. "We weren't expecting you so early."

"Could you keep an eye on Dayne, for just a few minutes?" Grayson sidestepped her.

"Sure." Rachel made a hasty retreat. "I'll just be out front."

Grayson waited until the door shut to speak. "You look like you've been crying."

"The arrangement always makes me sad."

"You're crying for Sara?"

"And for you and Dayne. Since the accident, the roses always make me a bit somber. Even more so, now that I know the men she left behind."

"You cried before you knew us?"

"Many times. It's just so heartbreaking. I'd heard Helen speak of you so often. You had the perfect marriage and family. Then it all got ripped away. It's not fair. . . ."

No need to tell him. Grayson knew firsthand just how heartbreaking and unfair his situation.

"No, it isn't. I appreciate your compassion."

Adrea added a whisper of baby's breath to the spray. "They're finished. I'll help you carry them to the car. Are you parked out front?" She picked up the white roses.

Grayson took the flowers but set them back on the counter. "I'm sorry I make you sad."

"Don't worry about me. Are you parked out front?"

"I'm afraid I can't do that."

"What?"

"Not worry about you."

His words robbed her of the ability to speak. Then she realized, it was the pastor's job to worry about his flock.

The showroom door opened to reveal Sylvie. "Fancy running into you here, Pastor. One of the salesclerks said you were here, just when I need a big strong man to carry my fern to the car. You wouldn't happen to have another, would you?" Sylvie's expression filled with pity. "Adrea dear, are you all right?"

"I'm fine. There should be two others out front. Unless they sold this morning. I can order more." *What's she up to?*

"It must be such a shock." Sylvie planted herself between Grayson and the door. "I mean, a mere two years ago, you were all set to marry Wade."

A sick feeling boiled in Adrea's stomach. Her mouth went dry. Grayson shot her a concerned look.

"Thank goodness you didn't marry him." Sylvie patted Adrea's arm, as if she genuinely felt sorry for the younger woman's plight. "I heard he fathered an illegitimate baby, but the mother took off. So I guess Helen will never see her grandchild."

Adrea cleared her throat. "Actually, the baby died."

"I hadn't heard that." Sylvie frowned, disappointment evident. *Less to gossip about.*

"Sylvie." Grayson used a warning tone.

"It's such a shame he reacted so badly to the breakup. Why, wasn't Valentine's Day supposed to be the wedding day?"

All color drained from Grayson's face. Adrea had expected the reaction, only it should have been after *she* told him.

"Oh my, you don't suppose our dear Sara got caught in the crossfire?" Sylvie gasped and drew a palm to her mouth.

"I'll escort you out, Sylvie." Grayson took her by the elbow. She flashed a victorious smile at Adrea.

An hour later, Grayson parked at the cemetery.

Adrea's car was already there.

It didn't surprise him.

With each step, his shoes sank into the soft earth. He trekked the familiar path to Sara's grave. From a distance, he could see Adrea kneeling, both hands covering her face.

At his approaching footsteps, she mopped the tears.

Noodle legs threatened to give way. Thankful for the shade of a sycamore tree, he sank to the white iron bench he'd bought last spring. "Tell me all of it."

"What's the point?" She shrugged.

"I need to hear it from you. I suspected you were once engaged to him."

Her eyes widened. "How?"

"Before Wade went into Mission 3:16, he said something that sounded like more than you simply working for his mother. I knew he was engaged a few years back and that it fell apart, so with the incident at the shop, I put it all together."

She sighed, as if the weight of the Ozark Mountains lay heavy on her shoulders. "When I first started working at the florist, Wade was in Little Rock, drinking a lot and Helen constantly worried about him. By the time we met, he'd been in several rehabs, joined AA, and had been sober for two years."

A robin burst into joyous song, oblivious to the somber mood.

"So she introduced you, a good Christian girl, to straighten him out."

Adrea nodded. "She invited me to tea at her house, and he happened to be there. Then, she tormented him until he came to a cookout at my church."

"And?"

"Wade rededicated his life to Christ. He was like a different person then. Very charming. We had a lot in common and wanted the same things."

"You loved him?"

"Yes." Her tears came again. "We had such plans. Building a house, starting a family, all the things I've longed for."

"Why the breakup?"

Adrea looked off in the distance, her eyes unfocused. "He wasn't convicted on some things. After our engagement, he. . ."

"What?"

"He wanted to be. . .intimate, before the wedding." A blush washed over her sensitive skin.

"I see." His stomach turned.

"But, we didn't. I tried to show him the verses in the Bible about such things, but it's like he didn't want to see it."

"So, that's why you broke up with him?" Relief bubbled through him. "Because he pressured you?"

Adrea plucked a piece of lush grass and twirled it between her fingers. "Two weeks before the wedding, Wade was upset because I couldn't have dinner with him on his birthday. I had two weddings and a funeral, but I managed to finish up earlier than expected and decided to go to his apartment to surprise him."

"And?" Grayson prompted.

"Um. . .he wasn't alone." She blushed again.

"I see."

"Of course, he said she meant nothing to him."

"You must have been very hurt."

She nodded. "I called off the wedding and Wade started drinking, on what should have been our wedding day. Valentine's Day."

He shuddered. "Adrea, it wasn't your fault. The only one at fault was Wade. You didn't put the bottle in his hand."

"I might as well have. If I'd married him, Sara would be alive and Wade would be fine."

He touched her forearm and offered his hand.

She settled on the bench beside him. "You don't under-stand. He ran the red light because he was drunk. Because *I* broke up with him. That's why Sara died."

Gently, he placed both hands on her shoulders.

Shocked at his touch, her eyes met his.

"Let's get one thing straight. You had no part in Sara's death or Wade's condition."

She didn't respond.

"You were right in breaking off the engagement. He cheated on you. And besides that, he's the one who made the decision to get drunk and then get behind the wheel."

He caught a tear as it trickled down her cheek. "What started Wade drinking this last time? Do you know?"

"He confessed to his pregnant fiancée about Sara. She aborted his baby."

Grayson's gut clenched. How could anyone do such a thing? *Concentrate on helping Adrea.* "So, it was her fault he started drinking again."

"Of course not."

"Why not? If the accident is your fault, then this other girl must be responsible for this binge. If he'd killed anyone this time, it would've been her fault. We might as well blame her for his attempted suicide, too."

Adrea shook her head. "Even though I don't condone what she did, you can't blame Shell for any of this. I mean, she's never been my favorite person, but Wade's bad choices aren't her fault."

"Then I'm at fault for his suicide attempt. Meeting me pushed him over the edge."

"No, you can't think that."

"Why? If the accident was your fault?"

She grasped his meaning and her eyes lit with hope.

Point made, he let go of her. "I'm sorry he caused you so much heartache. But no more guilt about this; you're not to blame."

"I was with him, just before he shot himself." She swallowed hard. "After you and Mark left, he ran out of the church and took Helen's car. She asked me to follow him, so I did. He told me about the accident and his confession, then promised to turn himself in. When I was leaving, I heard the shot. I found him."

"I heard." He cupped her face in his hands. "I'm so sorry."

"I shouldn't have left him alone. I should have sensed his plans."

"Stop taking the blame for things he did that you couldn't have stopped if you'd tried."

She nodded.

His hands dropped away from her.

"I should have told you. I'm sorry you had to hear it from Sylvie."

"Your past is really none of my business." He wanted it to be, along with her future, but he couldn't take the risk.

She swallowed hard. "I hope Sylvie won't tell Helen about the baby. Wade planned to marry Shell, then tell her."

"I'll have a talk with Sylvie. We need to have a discussion anyway."

She stood. "I need to get back to the shop."

"I'll walk you to your car."

"I'm fine. Really." She hurried away.

He wanted to follow, but his feet wouldn't obey. He dug a handkerchief from his pocket and wiped the dust off Sara's headstone, until the marble shone like polished glass.

⋧

On Sunday, with Mark handling the sermons, Grayson sat beside Helen, with Adrea seated on the other side of her. His attentiveness to Wade's grieving mother increased Adrea's respect for him.

A hush hung over the congregation. Not everyone knew of Wade's confession, but everyone seemed to feel the tension. After the altar call and closing prayer, Mark turned the service over to Grayson.

"I have an announcement to make." He took a deep breath. "As many of you know, Sara's case has been solved."

Audible gasps moved across the congregation and then shushed whispering.

"An individual came forward to claim responsibility. Police checked out his story, and it will hit the papers tomorrow. Helen and I want you to hear it from me." Grayson swallowed. "Wade Fenwick was responsible for the accident."

More gasps and whispers.

Adrea squeezed Helen's hand.

"Helen wanted to leave the church, but I hope I've changed her mind." He rested his hand on the older woman's shoulder. "It's been rough, but we're supporting one another and relying on God to get through this. We both need everyone's love and prayers and we don't need any gossip."

Maybe it was Adrea's imagination, but Grayson's eyes seemed to pause on Sylvie Kroft for a moment. The redhead looked down.

One of the deacons came to Helen and hugged her. Other members followed suit.

Tears blurred Adrea's vision at the show of Christian love for a wounded member of the body of Christ.

ða

July 4th, one of the biggest days for the shop. Red, white, and blue carnations perfumed the air. As she completed the fifteenth patriotic arrangement, the showroom door opened.

"Adrea?"

She jumped at the sound of Grayson's voice. Heart thumping, she turned to see him standing behind her. "Did I forget an order?"

"No." Grayson buried his nose in a lush, lacy red blossom. "But these are lovely, as usual."

"It's a very busy day." Adrea turned away, hoping he'd take the hint.

"I wanted to talk to you."

"Oh," she squeaked.

"Adrea, let me be honest with you." He paused a moment, as if gathering courage. "Since the day we met, I've spent an inordinate amount of time thinking about you. As we spend more time together, getting to know each other, I think about you even more."

"Oh," she echoed herself, again unable to form more than the single intelligible word.

"I haven't thought of anyone other than Sara for years, but recently a raven-haired beauty, with the darkest blue eyes I've ever seen, occupies my thoughts."

"I'm sorry." Stupid, but the only thing she could think of to say.

"Don't be. I thought when we were first getting to know one another that you might be interested in me as more than a pastor. But then you began trying to avoid me until Helen's injury and Wade's confession."

I tried, but you always managed to show up. Her brain caught up with him and the meaning of his words sank in.

"I avoid you, because thinking of you as only my pastor is difficult."

"Good, we're on the same page." The tension eased from his face. "It's strange. The confession opened up wounds, but it also gave me closure. With Sara's killer off the streets, I feel I can move on. You said it yourself; Sara would want me to be happy. Taking you out to dinner tonight would make me very happy."

"Okay." Her voice quivered. "But can we make it another night?"

"You have plans?" Disappointment resonated in his tone.

"No, not at all. It's just a really busy day here. I'll probably have to work late."

"I'll wait."

And she knew he would. Her heart fluttered.

"This may sound crazy." He grinned. "But I feel the need to be at ease. Some fancy place would probably make me nervous. How about Colton's Steakhouse over in Searcy?"

She grinned. "Sounds great. But what about Dayne?"

"Grace and Mark are taking him to a fireworks display at Harding University. I'll pick you up at seven o'clock? Is that late enough?"

"Perfect." *In every way.*

Grayson brought the back of her hand to his lips. "See you tonight."

Her breath hitched and shivers danced over her skin.

Barely able to function, she heard the showroom door open and close.

"What was that all about?" Rachel's words interrupted Adrea's thoughts.

"Nothing."

"Don't 'nothing' me." Rachel flashed a knowing smile. "It was definitely something."

"Why do you say that?"

"Because he's been coming here for over six years, but today, he asked to see you. And you're positively radiant." Rachel pointed a long-stemmed red mum at her. "Mum's the word. I'll even think of something to tell the salesclerks. They're busy with other customers, but curious. Now, spill."

Her face warmed. "As a matter of fact, we're going out to dinner tonight." Adrea stuck a leftover blue carnation behind her ear.

"Well, glory be." Rachel clapped her hands.

"What should I wear when going on a date with my pastor?"

"Hmm. Been there, done that. I can provide excellent advice."

❧

The humid weather dictated Adrea's attire. Wearing jeans and a purple top, she was glad to see that Grayson had dressed equally casual in an emerald button-down shirt—the exact color of his eyes—and khakis. Grayson Sterling had her full attention.

Peanut shells crunched beneath the server's feet as she brought their meal. Rawhide curtains graced the windows, with stuffed deer heads and razorback hogs mounted on the walls.

Grayson asked the blessing, then cut into his steak.

"Tell me how you and Sara met."

He paused to refold his napkin. "You really want to know?"

"If you don't mind talking about it."

"I can't remember my life before Sara." Grayson cleared his throat. "We lived in the same neighborhood. She and Grace were friends from the time they were toddlers, and we all went to the same Searcy school from kindergarten to graduation.

Sara was just my sister's friend, until we all turned sixteen. Out of the blue, I realized she didn't seem like a little girl anymore."

"So the two of you shared a lifetime together, which made losing her doubly hard."

He touched her hand. "You're incredible. Most women would be uncomfortable talking about my wife on a first date."

His simple touch turned her pulse erratic. "Sara will always be a part of you. You loved her and still do. I understand that and it doesn't bother me. So, did you always know you'd be a pastor?" She took a bite of her loaded chicken. *Mmm. Bacon, cheese, and mushrooms.*

"God called me to preach during my senior year. Sara went off to college and I enrolled at seminary." He paused to wash down the steak with sweet tea. "We married about a year later. She never got her teaching degree. When she got pregnant with Dayne, she quit, which was exactly what her parents feared. We planned for her to go back to school eventually and finish, but she never got that chance."

"She was happy without it."

Grayson looked at her, his eyes full of questions.

"According to Helen, and I could tell by the picture of her. Contentment radiated from her."

"Where did you see a picture?"

"In the newspaper."

"Oh, I'd forgotten." He traced the trickles of condensation on his glass with a fingertip. "Those days are still a fog for me."

"Over the years, I prayed for you and Dayne. I actually visited her grave once."

"You did?"

"Just the one time, a few days after we met. I couldn't get Sara off my mind. Then, I ran into you and Dayne in the park. Afterward, I ended up at the cemetery."

"Wow." His voice was barely a whisper.

"Sara's parents didn't hold it against you that she didn't finish college, did they?"

"Eventually, they realized Sara was happy as a wife and

mother. We all thought she'd have plenty of time for college later." He looked past Adrea, lost in thought for a moment. "I'm sorry."

"For what?"

"This is our first date. I didn't mean to talk about Sara tonight."

Adrea placed her hand over Grayson's and her heart raced again. "Don't apologize. I asked."

"Most women wouldn't be so gracious. I knew you were special the first time we met. I can't tell you how relieved I was to learn that Mark was your brother and not your husband."

"You had all kinds of misconceptions, didn't you?" As an excuse to move her hand and calm her heart rate, Adrea took a long drink of iced tea. "Mark and I were the last ones in the nest, after Rachel married, so we grew especially close. Once I graduated from high school, we got the apartment together. For two years, we relied on one another."

"Then Mark left for seminary in Memphis. Must have been hard on you."

"Even though he came home most weekends, it was a lonely four years. What about your parents?"

"Dad pastors at Thorndike here in Searcy." Grayson pushed his salad plate away. "So, did you always want to be a florist?"

"Actually, I wanted to be a vet, but I knew seeing hurt animals would tear me apart, so I settled for my second love of flowers."

"And your favorite is?"

"Yellow roses."

Something near the door caught Grayson's attention. "Great."

eight

Adrea looked up to see Sylvie Kroft and two new ladies from church. Shaking her head, Sylvie drew her new friends into a huddle.

"I guess my little project didn't work." Grayson shook his head.

"What project?"

"I asked Sylvie to print up two hundred Church Covenant cards, including the part about abstaining from backbiting."

Adrea pushed her plate away. "I'd really like to go."

"Don't let her ruin our evening," Grayson said.

"I'm not. I'm stuffed and you're finished. I thought we might catch up with Dayne and watch the fireworks display."

"He'd love that." He pulled out his wallet and laid several bills on the table.

Adrea waited while he paid; then they stepped out into the humid evening. Again, Grayson took her hand in his and drew it to his mouth. As his lips brushed her skin, fireworks lit the sky. Just like the ones bursting in her heart.

❧

It was a funeral day. But Mrs. Haynes knew the Lord, her children were grown and settled, and she'd longed to meet her deceased husband in glory. That knowledge helped Adrea.

With the rush of Independence Day orders over, Rachel had time to hang out in the workroom. "So did he kiss you?"

"On the hand."

"That's all?"

"It was very sweet."

"Dating a preacher is kind of weird. I mean, they're still men, you know."

Adrea relived the tingling sensation that had moved up her arm at the soft caress of his lips. "He's definitely a man. I'll

111

admit, I looked forward to more than a kiss on the hand."

"So, you just ate and talked?"

"Afterward, we went to watch the fireworks."

"Ooh, romantic."

"We met Dayne, Mark, and Grace there. Besides, half the town showed up."

"Leave it to my sister to squelch the romance." Rachel rolled her eyes.

"It was nice, and Dayne loved it."

Rachel checked her watch. "Time to open. I'd better go unlock the door."

While working on the casket spray, Adrea hummed "Blessed Assurance." A few minutes later, Rachel returned, holding a long white box tied with yellow ribbon.

"What's that?"

"The competition sent you flowers."

As Adrea took the box, she noticed that it came from Crissy's, a florist in Searcy. Anticipating the contents, she removed the ribbon and gasped at the dozen yellow roses inside. Catching her breath, she read the card:

> *Sorry, I had to use the competition. Your favorite flower seems to imply I'm interested in only friendship. The complete opposite is true.*

Adrea smiled, but a niggling doubt tumbled in her stomach. "Do you think it's too soon?"

"That's a hard question." Rachel added a few more red carnations to a casket spray. "Different people heal at different rates. Old Mr. Adams married six months after his wife died and nobody thought a thing of it."

Adrea finished the final spray for Mrs. Haynes by weaving a red ribbon through the carnations and lilies. "It's been almost two and a half years since Sara died."

"Just don't let what other people think determine your life for you." Rachel filled a tall crystal vase with water and put the yellow roses in it. "Let God determine if this thing with you and Grayson is right. As much as you two have been through, you both deserve happiness. And if you can take the tatters Wade left in his wake and mend it together, I say go for it."

"I just wonder sometimes if Grayson is really ready to move on. I mean emotionally."

"Apparently, he thinks he is. Just follow his lead."

Over the next few weeks, most of the new couple's dates included Dayne and sometimes they borrowed Haylee. They enjoyed family gatherings at the apartment, barbecues and picnics, the stuff of Adrea's dreams. Though, the events took place on the apartment lot, instead of in a backyard.

At church, Adrea realized she and Grayson were a hot topic. A few bolder members of the flock congratulated the couple. At least some people approved.

For Adrea's birthday, August 15th, Grayson invited her to his house for dinner for the first time.

"You have to see my room, Adrea," Dayne piped up from the backseat.

"I can't wait. I used to play in these woods with Mark and the Williams' grandson." As they turned into the long, winding drive, Adrea's childhood memories swirled.

Grayson winced. "It's probably not the eyesore you remember. The Williamses had gotten too old to take care of it. The men at the church have helped Grace and me transform it since we moved in."

"I've always loved this house. Even in disrepair, it always had such charm."

"Grace wanted to have you and Mark over long before now, but she's so busy with her business."

A freshly painted white fence flanked each side of the road for about a hundred yards; then the dense forest faded into a rounded clearing on one side. The stream, with a footbridge and ornate, white iron furniture nearby, gave her imagination flight. A lovely spot for a flower garden.

The second clearing revealed the two-story house. Huge

columns pillared the porch, which spanned the entire length. It looked like an old-South plantation. A picket fence enclosed the front and back yards. Perfect. For kids, cats, and dogs.

"Can I have a complete tour? I've always wanted to see the entire house."

"Sure."

A dog's bark echoed from the backyard.

"Can I go play with Cocoa?" Dayne called, an afterthought as he ran toward the side of the house.

"Don't get too dirty."

A spacious living room, large family room, cozy kitchen and dining area, four bedrooms, and two baths. The house boasted numerous windows, high ceilings, and walk-in closets.

Rendered speechless by the beauty of it all, Adrea finally found her voice. "It's the most beautiful house I've ever seen."

"You really like it, don't you? Grace hates it and Sara would've, too." He stared out the kitchen window. "It felt odd buying something she'd hate with her life insurance money, but Dayne loves it and we needed a new start, without all the memories."

"I've always wanted to fix up an old place. Just think of the history and lives lived here." She hugged herself.

"It's really too big for us, but I fell in love with it. I've always loved big, old houses. It took a lot of work, but it's been worth it. We have five acres with a walking trail around the property."

She looked out the sliding glass doors to see a deck across the back. Cocoa danced along a fenced enclosure as Dayne ran toward the house.

A garden, plenty of room for lots of pets, and a real backyard. Heat crept up her neck. *What am I thinking? We've only been dating a month.*

Dayne burst through the back door and grabbed Adrea's hand. "Come see." The boy propelled her down the hall.

His red and blue room housed every airplane imaginable, from the wallpaper and ceiling fan to his bedspread and curtains. Every piece of furniture and fabric resonated BOY. The small perfume bottle he retrieved from his chest of drawers went against everything else in the room.

"This was my mommy's." He held it up for Adrea to sniff. "Daddy lets me keep it so I can smell it when I miss her."

Adrea's eyes burned. The soft, powdery fragrance of flowers captured the essence of what she knew of Sara.

"It smells really pretty." She hugged him and blinked away the moisture. "I'm glad you have it to help you remember her."

Dayne inhaled deeply. "When I smell this, I can almost 'member sitting in her lap."

Unwilling to sadden the boy further, Adrea's tears fell as she turned away. "I really like your room."

⁂

"Don't worry. They'll love you." Grayson escorted Adrea up the sidewalk toward a white two-story house in Searcy.

Meeting his parents? Don't read too much into it.

His mother, Emma, met them at the door. "Come in. Come in." Her green eyes twinkled, just like her son's. Graham was a silver-haired version of Grayson.

They welcomed her into their large, inviting, older home. Dinner conversation consisted of theological studies. Just like spending time with Mark and Grayson. She willed her heart to slow.

After the meal, Emma gave Adrea a tour of her lovely garden. A lavender clematis vine snaked up a white lattice archway at the entrance of a floral wonderland. A natural rock border lined the flower beds, packed deep with cedar chips. Humongous hibiscus in pale pink and lilac mingled with purple and fuchsia petunias. The whir of hummingbird wings and buzz of honeybees formed an intense rivalry over various blossoms.

"I'm so happy Grayson is finally seeing someone." Emma held both of Adrea's hands in her own as the two women faced each other. "You don't know how we've worried about that boy.

"After Sara's death, at times we wondered if he'd ever

manage to keep on living. We never thought he was suicidal," Emma clarified. "Nothing like that, but he just lost his spark. For the last two years, he's only gone through the motions of life, for Dayne's sake. Then that drunk coming forward opened the tragedy all up again."

Adrea swallowed hard. "I guess Grayson told you about my connection to that drunk."

"The way I see it, you were another broken spirit left in the wake of Wade Fenwick." Emma hugged her. "For the last several months, Grayson has had the spring back in his step. Thank you for putting it there."

"Dayne and Grayson have been a blessing to me, too."

"God has brought healing to your and Grayson's souls by bringing you together. God is smiling on me." Emma winked. "First, he brings us Mark for Grace, and now, you for Grayson and Dayne."

"Oh, I don't know. We've only been seeing—"

Grace opened the patio door.

A green hummingbird with a splash of red across its throat flitted away.

"We need you two. Hurry up." Grace motioned them inside.

The three women hurried to the living room where they found the men.

"We have something to celebrate." Mark looked as if he might burst.

Adrea had a sneaking suspicion at the cause of her brother's happiness.

"Grace has agreed to marry me!"

"Whoo-hoo!" Emma threw her arms around her daughter.

"I'm so happy for you!" Adrea hugged her brother. "Have you told Mom and Dad? Mom will be beside herself."

"We're going there in a few minutes," Grace said.

Grayson hugged Grace. "Finally, you're getting a life of your own. That's some surprise."

"I feel guilty for abandoning you and Dayne. We're talking about several months away though, maybe New Year's Day."

And I can still watch Dayne after school and in the summers. I just won't live in that old relic with you anymore."

"Don't think of anything other than your happiness. Dayne and I will be just fine. We'll miss you, but if you want to get married next weekend, do it. Don't worry about us." He lowered his voice. "It's possible the Sterling household will change before long anyway."

Adrea gasped.

Grace, the only one who'd heard, stared openmouthedly, but left her inquiries unsaid.

He put his arm around Adrea's shoulders. "We better get Dayne home."

"Oh, but it's not even dark yet," Emma said.

"Yes, but he skipped his nap today, and he starts school next week."

☙

A few weeks later, Grayson and Adrea took Dayne to see a kiddie movie at the Rialto. Afterward, on the way to Romance, Grayson stopped at the coffee shop on the outskirts of Searcy. They entered the dimly lit café, and Adrea tried to adjust her eyes.

"Let's go somewhere else," Grayson whispered.

Confused, Adrea turned back toward the door.

As Grayson hurried them outside, she caught a glimpse of a middle-aged couple adding cream and sugar to their drinks. Somehow, they looked familiar to her, but she couldn't put her finger on how she might know them. It hit her as Grayson drove away.

"Where are we going, Daddy?"

"You ate such a good supper, let's go to the ice-cream shop instead."

The child didn't argue with that idea.

After Yarnell's Death-By-Chocolate ice cream, they arrived back at Adrea's apartment. Dayne went to the bathroom to wash his sticky hands.

"That was them, wasn't it?"

"Who?" Grayson's attempt to sound casual miserably failed.

"Sara's parents."

"How did you know?"

"I've seen their picture at your house and besides, she's an older version of Sara. They don't know about me, do they?"

"I'm sorry, Adrea." He hung his head.

"Don't be."

"I've ruined our evening."

"No you haven't."

"I just can't find the words to tell them. But I will. Soon." He clasped her open palm to his lips. "I promise."

❧

September 21st dawned a lovely day, Dayne's sixth birthday, his third without his mother.

Outside, birds chattered as if it were still spring. The showroom door opened and Grayson arrived just as Adrea finished the roses. "Beautiful as usual. This ritual doesn't bother you now that we're dating, does it?"

"Of course not. You know I'm okay with Sara's memory. Where's Dayne?"

"He's entertaining Rachel and the salesclerks. Would you like to come with us to the cemetery today?"

She opened her mouth, but no words came. Her heart hammered.

"Dayne and I discussed it already, and he said it was all right with him."

"Oh, Grayson, I couldn't possibly do that."

"Why not? We'd both like for you to come."

"I'd feel like such an intruder."

"You wouldn't be." He tipped her chin up with his fingers until she looked at him. "You've been there with me before, on Sara's birthday."

"Yes, but it was an accident and I felt terribly awkward."

The showroom door opened and Dayne entered.

"Dayne, I told you to wait out front."

"I know, but I wanted to ask Adrea. Are you going with us?"

How could she turn him down?

"You betcha. Happy sixth birthday, Dayne."

"Thanks."

"Just let me tell Rachel I'm leaving."

Dayne wriggled his little hand into hers.

Her heart warmed.

"I already told her." He tugged her toward the door.

Along with the curious salesclerks. "Let's go out the back." To avoid watchful eyes.

Soon, they reached their destination. The threesome held hands as Dayne carried the white roses for his mother. A blue jay squawked his disagreement with their presence. A squirrel grasped a hickory nut with both paws and chattered at them, then scampered up a tree.

They made the silent trek through the cemetery, side-stepping occasionally to avoid walking on graves.

In the few months they'd dated, her relationship with Grayson had deepened considerably. She knew for certain that she loved him, completely and irrevocably.

Grayson seemed to feel the same way.

She knew down to her toes, he was the one. No matter what anyone else thought, there was just something right about her and Grayson.

Though she'd loved Wade, she'd never had that right feeling with him.

"We don't talk to her at the cemetery," Grayson explained as they drew close to Sara's grave. "She's not here. We simply place the flowers to honor and remember her."

Dayne solemnly placed the flowers and polished the headstone while his father tidied up around the grave.

Adrea stood off to the side, still feeling a bit awkward, careful not to tread on Sara's memory.

♦

Since it was Saturday, the entire Sterling family, along with Adrea, Mark, and Haylee, gathered for lunch at Dexter's for Dayne's celebration. Sara's parents didn't show up, and Adrea knew it was because Grayson didn't invite them. Their absence bothered her, though she covered for Dayne's sake.

That night at Grayson's home, Adrea stood in the entryway,

staring at the table lined with Sara's image. Though Sara's face had embedded itself in her memory, she inspected the Sterling family portrait taken shortly before disaster struck. They looked so happy. The senseless tragedy still saddened her. Even though Adrea would have no place in Grayson's life if Sara were alive.

Sara had been a lovely woman. Her short blond hair, powder-blue eyes, and petite frame perfectly contrasted her husband's darker coloring. The two had been an attractive pair.

Strong arms came around Adrea's waist from behind. Though Grayson was careful not to hold her too closely, her pulse raced.

"I can put these away if they bother you."

"Don't you dare. They're lovely pictures of a happier time." She carefully set the gilded frame among the others on the marbleized tabletop.

"I'm quite happy right now. Thanks to you." He nuzzled Adrea's neck, sending shivers over her.

"I am, too, but you better stop that."

"Thanks for going with us today. I hope it wasn't too much for you."

"It was an honor that you wanted me to go." She wisely pulled away as he continued to cause shudders. "But it bothers me that you left Sara's parents out of today. I could have stayed home, for Dayne's sake."

"We had a party at their house yesterday, after school. Dayne thought it was cool to have two celebrations." Grayson turned her to face him, his hands resting on her shoulders. "They're coming for dinner next week, and I plan to tell them about you."

"It doesn't matter to me whether they know or not. I just don't want them hearing it from someone else."

"The movie's ready," Dayne called from the next room.

Linking his fingers with hers, Grayson pulled her to the family room.

Adrea expected a cartoon, but Sara's face filled the screen.

The camera panned out to show a birthday party for Dayne in a contemporary kitchen with stainless-steel appliances. Sara led several children and adults singing "Happy Birthday." The high soprano lilt of her voice riveted Adrea. Grayson apparently had filmed the video, as he wasn't in the happy scene.

Dayne sat in the floor, mesmerized by the image of his mother.

"That's the wrong tape, Dayne," Grayson said gently. "Turn it off and find the movie. We can watch that later if you want."

"We can watch it now if you like." Adrea's voice cracked. "We'll have plenty of time for the movie afterward."

"Are you sure?" Grayson mouthed silently.

She nodded and turned her attention back to the screen. The happy images of Sara trying to encourage a much younger Dayne to make a wish and blow out his candles made Adrea smile.

The scene changed to a backyard of a modern house. Children played numerous games with gleeful howls and giggles. She recognized most of the adults and children from church. While Grayson occasionally offered direction from behind the camera, Sara played referee. The tape ended with a shot of the entire group.

The happy faces of Sara's parents haunted Adrea. Tears trickled down her cheeks.

Quickly, she wiped them away. "Which birthday was that, Dayne?" The banner above the table, in the cake scene, proclaimed it his third. But maybe Dayne needed to voice his memories.

"I was three. It was my last birthday party with Mommy."

"From the tape, it looked like a good one."

"Why are you crying, Adrea?" Dayne asked. "You didn't know her, did you?"

So much for hiding tears. "No, but I've heard wonderful things about your mommy. It makes me sad that you and your daddy lost her."

Dayne ran to Adrea and hugged her. "It makes me sad, too, but I like 'membering her."

"I think that's enough sadness and *re*membering for one night. Let's watch the movie," Grayson suggested.

As Dayne pulled away and settled back on the floor, Grayson moved closer to Adrea on the couch and took her hand in his.

Halfway through the cartoon, she went to the kitchen to check on the slow-cooker.

A few minutes later, she looked up to see Grayson leaning in the door frame.

She shooed him away. "Go watch the movie with him. I can handle things here."

He stepped close and cupped her face in his hands. "I love you."

Tears welled in her eyes. "I love you, too."

Grayson kissed her soundly, then headed back to the family room.

Her heart skittered in her chest.

The doorbell chimed. With the cartoon on in the back of the house, Grayson probably wouldn't hear. Wooden spoon in one hand, she ran to open the front door.

A familiar couple stood on the porch.

Adrea pressed a hand to her heart. Its hammering echoed in her ears.

Obviously shocked, it took a moment before the woman spoke. "We're Dayne's grandparents, Joyce and Edward Owens. I didn't know Grayson had hired someone. I guess since Grace is getting married, she won't have as much time."

"Grandma! Grandpa!" Dayne zoomed into Joyce's waiting arms.

Adrea turned to see Grayson behind her.

"Joyce, Edward, what a surprise. It's great to see you."

His mother-in-law kissed him on the cheek. "You never told me you'd hired someone. I wouldn't mind bringing over a dish, and your mother would certainly do the same." Joyce turned back to Adrea. "Forgive me, dear. I don't mean to oust you out of a job."

Grayson cleared his throat. "I didn't hire anyone. Adrea is my—"

"Friend." Adrea's face warmed. "Everything is ready. Let me get the pork roast on the table and I'll be on my way. There's plenty for your guests."

"Dayne mentions you often." Edward's eyes narrowed. "You're his Sunday school teacher."

He knew.

"Dayne and I have become great friends." She hurried toward the kitchen.

"There's no need to rush off, Adrea. Why don't you join us?" Grayson followed her and lowered his voice. "Let me get it over with and tell them."

"There's no rush to do it tonight. Just have a nice dinner with them and I'll go." The haunting pain she'd seen in Joyce's eyes tore at her.

"I don't want you to go." Grayson kissed her.

Her heart did a somersault. "And I don't want to go, but they've been hurt enough."

"I planned to tell them next week. Now is as good a time as any."

"When it feels right, tell them." She set another place at the oak table. "Besides, my allergies are flaring up. I've sneezed several times and my throat is scratchy. I need some sinus medicine."

Before he could protest, she exited the kitchen and Dayne rushed into her arms. "You're not leaving, are you? I thought you were gonna eat with us."

"Not tonight, sweetie. We'll do it some other night. You enjoy visiting with your grandparents and I'll see you later."

❧

After Adrea left, the atmosphere didn't improve. At least Dayne seemed oblivious to the tension as the former family ate in silence.

Grayson watched his son consume his last bite. "Dayne, go put your pajamas on."

"But Grandma and Grandpa are here."

"Go get ready for bed; then you can visit."

"Okay." With slumped shoulders, Dayne hugged both his grandparents and went to his room.

"I know we saw Dayne yesterday." Edward inspected the intricate pattern on the handle of his fork. "But it just didn't seem right not seeing him on his birthday. We should have called."

"Is it serious?" Joyce's voice trembled as she pushed her plate away.

"What?" *That's it. Play dumb. Procrastinate.*

"Adrea. She's more than a friend."

"I'm sorry I haven't told you." Grayson folded his napkin and placed it over his uneaten food. "I just didn't know how to bring it up."

"How serious?"

"Joyce, it's none of our business," Edward cautioned.

"What affects Dayne is our business. How serious?"

Edward started to say something, but Grayson interrupted. "She's right. You both have a right to know. Eventually, I'll probably ask Adrea to marry me."

Joyce's chin quivered. She stood and ran from the room.

With an apology to Grayson, Edward followed.

❧

As soon as the Sunday morning service ended, Adrea hurried for the exit and hoped to slip past Grayson as he spoke with a young couple.

The man and woman left, just as Adrea reached him.

"I tried to call last night. I wish you hadn't left." Grayson's voice sounded strained.

"I went to bed early and Mark was out with Grace." She lowered her tone. "You didn't tell them, did you?"

"They figured it out."

"Were they upset?" Adrea looked around. Clusters of people dotted the sanctuary. Sylvie Kroft's stare bored a hole through her.

"Joyce was, but she'll get over it."

"We'll talk about it later. I have to go."

"I was hoping we could have lunch."

"Not today." She rushed out the exit and to her car.

Forty minutes later, she stood on the stone steps of the Owens' home. Three times, she'd gone to the polished oak door, then back to her car, then back to the door. She stood with her finger inches from the bell, but couldn't force herself to push it.

I shouldn't have come.

The door opened. She stood face-to-face with Edward Owens.

"Hello, I thought I saw someone out here."

"I found your address in the phone book. Is this a good time? If not, I understand completely." She turned toward her car.

"It's a perfect time."

"Are you sure?"

"Yes. We need to talk."

"Is your wife still upset?"

He nodded. "It's not your fault. Adrea? Is that right?"

"Yes."

"A unique name. I thought maybe Dayne was leaving the *n* off of Adrian."

"People often call me that."

"Dayne thinks the world of you."

"I adore him." Adrea pleated the folds of her skirt between thumb and forefinger. "Grayson has no idea I'm here. It seemed like a good idea for us to speak, but now it seems all wrong."

"Edward, is someone here?" Joyce called, just before she stepped into the open doorway. Dark circles under her eyes testified to a sleepless night. Her chin quivered.

"I'm sorry, I shouldn't have come." Adrea bolted.

"Grayson said the two of you are serious." Joyce barely got the words out.

Halfway to her car, Adrea stopped and turned to face Sara's parents. "This must be so hard for you. I thought it might help if you knew how much Grayson and Dayne mean to me. They"—Adrea searched for adequate words—"complete me. I love them both, very much."

"Please come inside." Edward beckoned to her. "We need to talk this out and we have rather a—" He gestured to the next house. "Rather an inquisitive neighbor, who should be home anytime."

"Are you sure?"

"Yes." Joyce nodded. "Please come in."

nine

Inside the house, pictures of Sara greeted Adrea. While Grayson had one tabletop filled with his wife's image, photos of Sara occupied every empty space on the wall and all flat surfaces in her parents' home. Sara as a fat, frolicking baby. As a wobbly toddler. In grade school, high school, college. Sara as a bride and a new mother, and then with a toddler of her own. The pictures abruptly stopped, as her life had.

"Dayne talks about you constantly." Edward gestured toward the overstuffed sofa.

She perched on the edge. "I love your grandson very much."

"Grayson said you'd been seeing one another a few months."

Adrea clasped her hands together, willing them to stop trembling. "They loved Sara long before they ever met me and they still love her. Grayson and I will never have what they had. If Sara were still here, Grayson would never have looked at me twice, and I'm okay with that."

Joyce's tears flowed freely now.

"I'm so sorry that this hurts you. Maybe it was wrong of me to come." Adrea started toward the door but stopped and turned back toward the Owenses.

"It's not fair. Sara should have lived to see Dayne grow up. She should have grown old with Grayson. I wish to the depths of my soul that she had, even though it would have changed the course of my life. But Grayson is ready to move on. He loves me, and Dayne loves me.

"Yet, it's not fair to you. You don't get to move on. Dayne and Grayson get someone new to love, but you can't get another daughter. And for that, I'm eternally sorry." Adrea hurried outside to her car.

With trembling fingers, she managed to start the engine.

She scanned the house next door. A head bobbed from the window and hid behind the swaying curtains. The red hair looked familiar. Sylvie Kroft.

❧

After evening services, Grayson caught up with her. "Where'd you run off to this morning? I tried to call several times."

"I went to see Sara's parents."

He cocked an eyebrow.

"I shouldn't have." Her hushed tones were for his ears only. "I rattled on and on. I should know by now that any bright idea that takes shape after midnight is a bad one."

"You tried to help and maybe you did. Maybe getting to know you will make them feel better." He grinned. "I honestly don't know how anyone could not like you."

Her heart warmed. "You're prejudiced."

"Definitely." He frowned. "You didn't mention Wade or your relationship with him?"

"No, I figured they could only handle one bombshell at a time."

A niggling unrest struck her in the gut, as if eyes bored into the back of her head. She turned to see Sylvie Kroft's contempt.

Adrea moved away from Grayson.

His gaze questioned her sudden need for escape.

Helen stopped her progress. "What a lovely arrangement. The two of you. It's perfect."

"I'm glad somebody thinks so." Adrea started toward the exit but remembered she'd left her lesson book in the children's classroom this morning.

She crossed the sanctuary and went downstairs to retrieve it. By the time she returned, the church had emptied. She heard voices coming from the lobby.

"I tell you," Sylvie hissed, "she's intent on replacing Sara, in every sense of the word."

Adrea peeked around the wall. The three women stood in a circle.

The kinder of the three, Mrs. Patton she'd learned, spoke

first. "I don't think so. They've both been through a lot, and I think it's wonderful if they can find some happiness together. Adrea seems like a real dear."

"Don't let her fool you." Sylvie paused to scan the length of the lobby.

Adrea flattened herself on the other side of the wall.

"First she took the children's class Sara used to teach. Then she took Sara's flower ministry. Now, she's set her cap for Sara's husband and child. Why, she visited Sara's poor grieving parents just this afternoon and tried to worm her way in with them."

Eavesdropping. *What have I lowered myself to?* The white silk roses with sprigs of freesia and Casablanca lilies sat in front of the pulpit. She'd lovingly arranged them to honor Sara.

Clearing her throat, she straightened her spine and walked casually through the lobby to the exit. "Evening, ladies."

She hurried outside, hickory nuts rolling, crunching, and popping with each step.

"There you are." Grayson waited beside her car.

"I forgot my lesson book in my class." Sounded almost natural.

"You okay?" With a furrowed brow, he touched her arm.

"Fine."

"Dayne went with Grace and Mark. How about we stop for coffee?"

"Not tonight." She opened her car door. "I'm tired."

"Edward called me a few minutes ago." He loosened his tie and ran his hand along the back of his neck. "He and Joyce invited us over for dinner next Thursday night."

"Us?" Her stomach twisted.

"They insisted on your presence. I hope you don't mind, but I suggested they come to my house instead. I thought you could cook a nice meal."

"Win them over with my culinary skills." A smile escaped. "You sound like my mother."

"Actually, I thought it would be good for them to see you

with Dayne and me at the house. The house where Sara never lived."

The wind gathered brown, curling leaves, rolling and scraping across the asphalt.

"I don't know." An engine started nearby. "School is out for parent/teacher conferences, and the kids are supposed to spend the night with Mark and me. We promised a hot dog roast."

"So, we'll move it to the house. Haylee can keep Dayne occupied while the adults talk."

Sylvie pulled out, without waving. Mrs. Patton waved, when her car passed, but Mrs. Hughes didn't.

Adrea shook her head. "Maybe this is all too soon."

With the parking lot empty, he pulled her into his arms. "Not for me. Please come."

In the comfort and security of his embrace, she'd agree to almost anything.

And he knew it.

Playfully, she slapped him on the back. "Oh all right."

※

Adrea straightened Sara's checked blanket across the redwood picnic table on Grayson's back deck.

"Look. A frog." Dayne held a large toad inches from her face. The creature lowered his warty head and blinked one eye at her.

She laughed "I think he just winked at me."

"You're not afraid of him?"

"I love frogs. When I was a kid, Daddy built my brother and me a frog cage. It had screen all around the sides. Mark put dirt, grass, and sticks in it so they'd feel at home. We kept a pan of water in the corner and spent hours swatting flies to feed them."

"Cool." Dayne petted the frog with one careful finger.

"We'd keep them for a while, then turn them loose and catch a new batch. Sometimes, we had twenty frogs at a time. Maybe we could talk your dad into building a frog cage." The lighthearted fun couldn't quell the knots in the pit of her stomach.

"I don't think so."

"Why not?"

"He's afraid of frogs."

"Your father is afraid of frogs?" Adrea couldn't suppress her laughter.

"Terrified. I love sticking them in his face. It makes him pretty mad. I figured you was afraid of them, too."

"What does he think a frog can do to him?"

"He says when they move their neck like that"—Dayne pointed to the creature's undulating throat—"they're working up a spit. I never had no frog spit on me, have you?"

She laughed so hard, the muscles in her stomach clenched. "No, I haven't."

"Dayne, haven't I told you not to touch those things?" Grayson set a huge pitcher of sweet tea on the table. "One of these days, one will spit on you."

"Adrea likes 'em, Daddy. When she was little, she had pet frogs and says they don't spit."

"She does, huh?"

"I'm gonna ask Mr. Theo to build me a frog cage." Dayne scurried away to show Haylee his prize.

Grayson cocked an eyebrow. "Frog cage?"

"Mark and I used to have one." She shrugged.

Dayne and Haylee chased Cocoa around the yard.

Adrea set the buns, mustard, and relish on the picnic table, with shaking hands.

"Calm down." Grayson stoked the fire. "They wanted you here."

A tingling, burning sensation assailed Adrea's nose and worsened with each breath. She grabbed a paper napkin. "Uh—uh—*achoo*."

"Bless you. That might be more than allergies. Maybe you should go to the doctor."

"Adrea, come help us," Dayne called.

The small plastic pool billowed bubbles. Not only was Cocoa in the makeshift bathtub, but both kids also, their teeth chattering.

"Dayne, I told you not to get in there." Grayson shook his head. "It's too cool and Grandpa and Grandma will be here any minute."

Adrea stifled her laughter and walked over to the kids. "You'll both need a bath."

"We'll take one here." Haylee scrubbed Cocoa's back with a brush.

"I don't think you'll get clean in this bathtub." Adrea surveyed the muddy water. "Okay, Cocoa, let's get you washed up and then the rest of us will go inside to freshen up."

Large, patient, brown eyes peered at her from the bubbles. The smell of wet dog surrounded them. Cocoa shook. Ears flapping, he doused everything within several feet with gritty water and soap. Adrea ducked as the chilly mess splattered across her.

"Dayne, get that dog out of the pool!" Grayson shouted.

Unable to contain her laughter anymore, Adrea gave up. She joined the muddy dog and children in the pool, with icy water up to her shins and teeth chattering.

Grayson's laughter roared across the yard.

Adrea noticed movement at the side of the house. Edward and Joyce.

The laughter died on Adrea's lips.

Following her gaze, Grayson's amusement instantly stopped as well.

"Grandma! Grandpa!" Dayne cried, leaping from the pool. The sopping boy ran toward his grandparents.

In spite of the muck, Edward hugged the child. "You're a mess."

"We're giving Cocoa a bath." At Dayne's words, the dog baled from Haylee's grasp, ran across the yard, and shook repeatedly. The adults tried to avoid the torrent, while the children cackled with glee.

Finally, Grayson caught Cocoa and Adrea supplied him with a somewhat dry towel.

"Okay, kids, inside and clean up, then we'll eat." Adrea herded them toward the house.

"You won't leave before I get back?" Dayne asked his grandparents.

"No, we'll be here." Edward squeezed the boy's shoulder.

"We're roasting marshmallows and making s'mores for dessert." Dayne jumped up and down.

"That sounds. . .cozy." Joyce tried to join in his excitement.

"Are you sure you won't leave?" Dayne pressed.

"I promise." Joyce stood firm, immovable. "We'll be right here."

æ

With Adrea and the kids out of earshot, Grayson shook Edward's hand and hugged Joyce.

"It's always nice to see you. I didn't like the way we left things the other night."

"We came to tell you that we've accepted the relationship." Joyce's voice quivered. "It's hard for us, but you've been lonely long enough." She cleared her throat. "Adrea is a wonderful woman. Seeing her with Dayne, just now, proved it."

"I truly love and respect you both and hate hurting you. I'm sorry."

"Don't be." Edward patted Grayson's shoulder. "You deserve happiness. Sara would want it for you, and she'd want someone to love Dayne, as well."

"I didn't know Adrea had a daughter." Joyce sounded stronger. "But the little girl and Dayne seem to get along well."

"Haylee is Adrea's niece."

"Oh. She was so caring with the child, I just assumed."

I did, too. Grayson grinned at the memory. "Adrea is great with kids. Dayne and Haylee are spending the night with Adrea and her brother tonight. They do that two or three times a month."

A polished Adrea emerged from the house, with a scrubbed Dayne and Haylee, all wearing fresh clothing.

"Thankfully, I just picked up my dry cleaning today and Haylee had clothes packed." Adrea seemed flustered, anxious to explain that she didn't keep clothes at the house.

Joyce took a deep breath and met Adrea on the sidewalk. "Take care of my boys." Joyce offered her hand.

"I will." Adrea accepted the bridge.

"You have my blessing."

Tears filled Adrea's eyes.

Grayson's heart swelled until he thought it might burst. Nothing stood between them now. With the blessings of everyone involved, she could become his wife. Why wait?

I'll ask her at dinner, tomorrow night.

જ઼

Adrea's stomach clenched. With a temperature of 101, the closer she got to the apartment, the darker the foreboding black cloud of smoke hovered in the sky. Surely, it couldn't be.

She topped the hill to see fire shoot from a downstairs window. The firefighters stood around their truck, barking orders, manning the hose.

With the parking lot blocked, she turned into the drive of the next house.

"Everyone got out," her elderly neighbor yelled. "Mark is at the church, right?"

She nodded. The knot in her gut eased.

From the sodden yard next door, Adrea watched the firemen make progress. The flames seemed contained downstairs, but the blaze wasn't under control. Mark's car careened over the hill and screeched to a halt.

Grayson lurched from the passenger's side and rushed toward the burning building. Her brother bolted toward the crowd. A firefighter caught Grayson and did his best to hold him back. With chaos and smoke surrounding her, Adrea pushed through the gathering crowd.

Mark saw her first. His eyes brimmed with tears as he pulled her into his arms.

"I just got here. I'm fine."

"We have to find Grayson." Mark kissed her forehead. "He's a mess."

Holding hands to keep from being separated, they made

their way through the pandemonium. Adrea recognized Grayson's dark hair and rushed up behind him. When he caught sight of her, his knees gave way. She knelt on the ground beside him as he moaned incoherently.

"I'm okay, Grayson. Don't worry. Everything is fine."

"Grayson, Adrea is right here. She's fine." Mark turned to her. "We need to get him out of here."

Adrea helped her brother pull Grayson to his feet and walk him back to the car. They settled the distraught man in the backseat, and she climbed in beside him. Grayson laid his head in her lap. Gut-wrenching sobs tore through him.

"Where are we going?" she asked.

"The church." Mark turned onto the highway.

They met another fire truck and it took longer than usual to get to their destination. Grayson was still beyond words as Adrea stroked his hair.

"How did you find out?" She directed the question to Mark.

"Peg heard it on the radio and came to tell us. Since we knew you stayed home sick today, we were both terrified."

"My fever wouldn't break, so I went to the doctor. Bronchitis."

By the time they arrived at the church, Grayson could walk by himself.

Peg, the secretary, rushed to meet them, obviously shaken at the sight of her shattered boss. "Is everyone okay?"

"No one was hurt in the fire, but it took us a little while to locate Adrea," Mark explained.

"Thank God no one was hurt. I'll get some coffee." Peg darted for the hall.

"Thanks." Adrea's voice was little more than a croak.

Mark's eyes were too shiny. "You may need to see your doctor again."

"I'm fine. The smoke irritated my throat since it was already raw from the bronchitis."

Grayson sat hunched over on the couch with his head in his hands.

Peg returned with coffee, creamer, and sugar, then left them alone.

"Well, we can stay in the basement here for a few days until we find a place to rent." Mark ran his fingers through his hair and paced, in fix-it mode. "We have a couple of cots for emergencies. Grace and I can go shopping and get us each a week's worth of clothing until we determine the damage. Write down your sizes for me. I'll call Mom and Dad, Rachel, and Grace to let them know we're okay. Peg is calling a few people from church."

"Make sure she calls Helen." Adrea never took her eyes off the distressed man at her side. "She's at the shop today."

"Grayson, are you all right?" Mark asked.

"Can you handle Sunday's sermons for me?" Grayson mumbled. "I don't think I'll be up to it."

Adrea blew out a breath, thankful to hear him speak.

"Sure."

"Thanks for getting me out of there, Mark. People didn't need to see the local pastor disintegrate."

"No problem. Everyone expects preachers to be made of steel, but we're only human. With everything you've been through, you had every right to fall apart." Mark gave her shoulder a gentle squeeze. "I'll be back soon."

As soon as the door closed, Grayson laid his head in Adrea's lap again. "I can't lose you, Adrea."

"You didn't. I'm fine."

"The mere thought of losing you was almost more than I could bear."

"You're fine. You just had a scare."

Disentangling himself from her arms, he sat up and wiped away the tears, then buried his face in both hands.

Adrea massaged his knotted shoulders.

"I have to pull myself together enough to pick Dayne up from Mom's. It's time for me to go." He sat upright next to her. "I don't think I can handle dinner tonight. I'm so tired."

"I'm not feeling very well anyway. Just take care of Dayne and go to bed early." Adrea traced his jawline lightly with her fingers and started to hug him again.

He quickly turned away from her and stood. Without another word, he left.

Her stomach tumbled.

❧

As Adrea made up her cot, footsteps echoed across the tile. She turned to see Grayson, his face haggard and drawn. Yesterday's fire seemed to have put ten years on him.

"I thought you might call last night." Her voice came out high-pitched.

"I meant to, but I fell asleep on the couch. Where's Mark?"

"He went to check out the apartment."

"Good, we need to talk."

"I'm worried about you."

He wouldn't look at her. Instead, he stared at the floor.

A chill skittered up her spine. She wasn't sure if it was from fever or apprehension.

He took a shaky breath. "Yesterday proved once and for all that I'm not ready for this."

"Ready for what?"

"To love someone so deeply that the thought of losing them cripples me. I can't do this again."

"Grayson, what are you saying?" Tentatively, she touched his forearm.

"We shouldn't see each other anymore."

"You're not thinking clearly. You just had a scare, but it's over now."

"I can't risk letting myself love like this again." He turned away from her. "With the possibility of losing again."

"That's life." Adrea spoke to his back. "You've said it yourself: God doesn't promise us how much time we have. We simply have to trust Him, live our lives, and to the best of our ability, glorify Him. He never promised it would be easy, just that He'd be there for the rough times, to hold us together."

"I'm sorry for leading you to believe we had a future together. Just be glad I figured out what a coward I am now, instead of later. I planned to propose to you last night."

His admission jolted through her. It should have filled her with joy, not sadness at all that she had to lose. An iron fist closed around her heart.

She stepped in front of him, forcing Grayson to look at her. "We *already* love each other. It's a little too late to decide you're not ready."

"I'm sorry for hurting you, but I can't open myself up to loss again." His shoulders drooped. "I barely made it the first time and don't have the strength for another round."

"You don't know what will happen. We may live to be a hundred, or you could die long before me. But eventually, we both get eternity. Let God give you the strength. You can't live in fear and close your heart."

"Dayne needs the only parent he has left to be strong and remain capable of functioning, for his sake." His gaze never left the floor.

"So, you're letting fear—of something that may never come—steal your happiness. 'For I the Lord thy God will hold thy right hand, saying unto thee, Fear not; I will help thee,'" Adrea quoted from Isaiah.

Grayson turned away from her again. "I'd rather not love than to love and lose again. I'm not the man you thought me to be. Forget about me; find someone else. You deserve happiness."

Shaking her head, she stiffened her spine and, with as much pride as she could muster, left the room. With nowhere to go, she ran to the fellowship hall and paced the length of the building until she heard a car start and leave. Through sheer willpower, she refrained from crying.

She pushed Grayson's mention of a marriage proposal to the back of her mind, refusing to allow herself to think about it now. She couldn't let the tears start, knowing they wouldn't stop. The emotional strain did nothing to ease her fever and throbbing head.

The door opened and she jumped.

"Whoa." Mark held both hands up, palms facing her.

"Don't go through yourself, it's just me. Good news. The flames never reached the upstairs. One of the firefighters told me the house is structurally sound. We probably sustained smoke and some water damage, but that's all. We should get the chance to see what's salvageable in the next few days."

Mark took in her appearance. "What's wrong?"

"Can we get a motel or something?" Her voice cracked.

"Sure, if you want to, but why?"

"Did you see Grayson when you came back?" she squeaked.

"No, his car is gone. What happened?" Worry formed on her brother's face in the shape of a frown.

The tears she'd been holding inside coursed down her cheeks.

"Hey, what's wrong?" Mark pulled her into the shelter of his arms.

"Grayson doesn't—want to—see me—anymore." Her hiccuped words ended on a sob.

"Why? He loves you."

Incapable of answering for several minutes, Adrea's tears soaked Mark's blue cotton shirt. Finally, she pulled away from him.

"The fire scared him and he's afraid he'll lose me. He said he'd rather not love than to love and lose again."

"That's the most ridiculous thing I've ever heard." Mark's eyebrows drew together. "He already loves you."

"That's what I said. He says he can't risk losing me."

"So he'd rather not have you at all?"

The tears began again.

He pulled her back into a comforting embrace.

"I can't stay here, Mark, and worry about running into him."

"How about Mom and Dad's?"

"Maybe tomorrow. I can't deal with everyone's sympathy right now. Please can we find a motel just for tonight, so I can try to pull myself together?"

"Sure." He squeezed her hand.

❧

An hour later, Adrea sat in a spotless Searcy motel, trying to pull herself together again.

Mark pressed his palm against her forehead. "You're burning up. Have you taken anything for that fever?"

"Not lately. I guess my antibiotics are still in the car."

"I'll go get your prescription. I bought some sinus medicine and aspirin along with the clothes." He disappeared into the bathroom and returned with a cup of water and the medicine. "Here, take these. I wish we had a thermometer."

Before leaving, Mark tucked her into her bed as he would a child. Within minutes, he was back with her antibiotics.

For hours, she tossed and turned. Knowledge of Grayson's intended proposal was something she could've lived without. Lying on her back, hot tears coursed down each side of her face, quickly soaking the hair at her temples. Crying swelled her sinuses even more, and she could only breathe through her mouth, which made her throat hurt worse. She rolled over and tried to mask her sniffles by burying her face in the pillow. Soft snoring came from the other queen-size bed; at least she wasn't keeping her brother awake.

When she finally did fall into a fitful sleep, dreams plagued her. Dreams of a raging fire keeping her from Grayson. No matter how hard she tried, she couldn't reach him. As the flames closed in on her, Adrea awoke with a start, drenched in sweat. At least her fever had broken.

⁊⍺

Saturday evening, on autopilot, Grayson didn't want to go to the church, but he had to check his messages and clear his calendar. Would Adrea attend tomorrow? Would he get through the service if she did?

At least there were no other cars in the lot, except Peg's.

She met him at the door. "Are you okay?"

Must have been watching for him. He knew she wasn't nosy, just genuinely concerned about him.

"I'm fine. Just tired."

"Coffee's brewing. I'll bring you a cup in a few minutes."

"That would be great, but I'll come get it. You don't need to wait on me. Really, I'm fine."

"I don't mind. Mark and Adrea got a motel, so they're gone."

Her name twisted the double-edge sword lodged in his chest.

"Thanks for letting me know." In his office, he leaned his elbows on the cool surface of the desk and covered his face with both hands. A few minutes later, he heard footsteps.

Expecting to see Peg, instead he looked up into the angry face of Mark.

Grayson stood to greet him, hand extended.

Mark slammed his fist into Grayson's midsection.

He bent double as breath escaped him.

"That's for Adrea." Mark muttered the unnecessary explanation and stalked down the hall.

Gasping for breath, Grayson followed, his stumbling footsteps echoing on the tile.

Halfway to the foyer, Mark turned to face him. "You want more?"

"No, though it is justified." Grayson strained to speak. "Adrea didn't deserve the way I treated her. I pursued her and then decided I couldn't take the heat."

"No pun intended," Mark referred to the fire, but his glare showed no trace of humor.

Mark's glare showed no trace of humor. "I never met a man worthy of my sister, until you. I encouraged your relationship, pushed you toward her. And what did you give me in return? You broke her already broken heart and turned your back on her when she was sick and suddenly homeless."

He couldn't argue with the truth. "I need some time off. Can you fill in for me, say for about a month?"

"You need some time off? What about Adrea? How do you think she feels?"

"Actually, it might help her if I disappear for a while."

Mark sighed. "Okay, but not for you. For her, and when you come back, prepare to find yourself another associate."

"Now, Mark, there's no need for that." Grayson shook his head. "You do a great job here. This doesn't have to affect our church relationship. Let's just forget that you winded me, especially since I deserved more."

"I don't think I can work with the coward who devastated my sister." Mark stalked to his own office.

Grayson didn't follow. He walked outside and tried to come up with an explanation for Dayne on why they needed to pack up and leave.

≈

Adrea didn't go to church. Guiltily, she slept in as October dawned, then met Mark at the abandoned apartment house.

"I'll probably smell smoke for the rest of my life." She sifted through their belongings, a pungent odor hanging heavily in the air.

"It could have been much worse." Mark swept a pile of sodden refuse into the corner. "We could have lost everything, including our lives. God blessed us, sis. No one was hurt and the damage was limited."

"Right again." She found their photo albums nestled in a dry corner and flipped through them. *Thank You, God.* "No more complaints from me."

"We should probably try to find a new place, though. The landlord said the smoke removal might take some time, along with the repairs downstairs. But, I have some good news."

"What?"

"Our not-so-fearless leader is leaving for a month. He feels the need for a sudden sabbatical."

Adrea's breath caught in her throat. *Concentrate on the effect of his absence on others.* "What about Dayne? School just barely started."

"Grace said he worked it out so Dayne can homeschool for the month. His teachers are sending all his schoolwork with them."

"What about the church?" She dropped some pictures, which had never made it out of the store envelope, into a box with the albums.

"I'm in charge until he returns. After that, I plan to look for a new church."

"Oh, Mark, don't leave Palisade because of me." She propped both hands on her hips. "God placed you there. Let Him decide when you need to leave. You have Grace to support you now, so I'm planning to return to Mountain Grove anyway."

Mark's jaw clenched. "I can't fulfill my calling under a man I no longer respect."

"You have to get past this. That man is your fiancée's twin brother. You're stuck with him. Do whatever you have to in order to work things out with him. Don't worry about me, I'll be fine."

Mark didn't respond and she dropped the subject, for now.

"Since we're basically homeless, we could move a little farther out of town." Farther away from Grayson. "We could get a smaller apartment. Your wedding's barely three months away, and I won't need as much space after you're gone."

"I won't allow you to run or go off on your own to lick your wounds." Mark touched her cheek with his fingertips. "We'll find something where we both can live happily and maybe you could move in with Grace and me after we're married."

"I'm not moving in with you and your bride." She turned away to dig through another pile.

"We can talk about all of that later. In the meantime, I may need your help charming my angry fiancée after she sees her brother."

Adrea whirled to face him. "What did you do?"

"It was no big deal."

"Mark? Did you hit him?"

"Nothing that will leave a mark." He smiled. "Pardon the pun."

"I'm not amused." She looked heavenward. "You are a preacher!"

ten

"It was righteous anger," Mark said.

"You really hit him?" *Please be joking.*

"Just in the stomach, but it took him a while to catch his breath. He's pretty solid. In fact, my hand still hurts."

"Mark!"

"I wanted to knock his head off, but that would cause a bruise and people would ask questions. This way, it was just between him and me." Mark dusted his hands against one another.

"And God—and Grace. How on earth did you preach this morning?"

"I felt great, until now." Guilt flattened Mark's voice.

She plopped into a chair. A smoky odor wafted from the fabric. "Listen to me. I am fine. I'll get over Grayson Sterling. Please don't let this affect your position or your relationship with Grace. You two love each other so much. I couldn't stand it if problems arose between you because of me."

"Grace and I will survive. Don't worry. We'll find another church."

She lifted an eyebrow. "You haven't spoken with her about this?"

"I didn't want to tell her on the phone. She's helping her marvelous brother get ready for his trip. By now, he's probably told her all about the wallop I delivered."

"He'd never do that."

"Why are you defending the man?" The veins in Mark's neck bulged.

Adrea closed her eyes. "Don't ask Grace to choose between you and her twin brother."

"If God calls me to another church someday, Grace will go with me, not stay at Palisade."

"This is different. When that happens, you'd leave because of God's will. If you leave now, you'll make the decision out of anger and force her to choose."

"She'll choose me," Mark mumbled.

"Are you certain? And even if she does, if you truly love Grace, you won't ask her to make that choice."

Mark ran a hand through his hair. "I belted the guy for your honor and you go and make me feel guilty."

"How would you like it if Grace asked you to choose between her and me?"

Mark sighed.

"Do whatever it takes to repair your relationship with Grayson." Adrea touched her brother's arm, desperate to communicate the importance of the situation. "If you want to do something for me, make amends. I didn't want you to hit him, but I want this."

🍃

Before Grayson left, Mark forced himself to bury the hatchet, though Adrea knew he wanted to bury it in the back of Grayson's head. Since Grace was a little miffed at her brother over his broken relationship with Adrea, she took the news of Mark's punch in stride.

After two weeks at Mom and Daddy's, Adrea and Mark stood with Rachel outside one of only two affordable rental houses in Romance. Nice, freshly painted, and well-kept—but directly across the street from Wade's old house. Where he'd lived during his and Adrea's relationship. Where they'd planned to begin their marriage. Where she'd caught him with another woman.

She tried to concentrate on October's vivid kaleidoscope of yellow, orange, and red leaves.

"We'll find something else." Mark ran a hand through his hair.

The chipper real estate agent pointed across the street. "Remember, that one's available also. Same owner."

"There's got to be somewhere else."

Wind chimes tinkled in the nippy wind. The ones she'd

bought Wade? "We'll take this one."

The woman grinned and handed her the key. She counted the cash Adrea gave her and turned toward her car. "If you need anything, don't hesitate to call."

Adrea blew out a big sigh and picked up a box, dug around in it until she found a pair of scissors, and marched across the street.

"What are you doing?" Rachel followed.

Adrea snipped the string holding the chimes. They clattered to the porch in a tangled heap.

"Brilliant. But I still can't believe you're taking the place."

"It's just a house." Unlike her sister, Adrea had long ago made peace with Wade, forgiven him, and even visited him at the nursing home in Searcy. Yet, she didn't need to go back. Only forward. To her side of the street.

"You don't hum or sing while you work anymore. How can you ever be happy living here, looking at that every time you step outside your door?" Rachel motioned at the house full of memories, then dug one of the plants that had survived the fire out of Mark's Tahoe.

"I'll heal. I plan to continue attending Palisade while he's gone. But in a few weeks when he comes back, I'll go back to Mountain Grove."

"Did you find someone to take your children's class?"

Adrea set a box of pictures in the living room. "Mrs. Roberts has recovered from her heart attack, but she felt my youth was good for the children and never reclaimed her post. However, with gentle persuasion, I'm sure I can talk her into teaching again."

"I'm sorry you're hurting, but it'll be nice to have you back at church." Rachel hugged her.

She'd miss the friends made at Palisade, and especially Helen. It seemed just weeks ago, she'd faced changing churches. So much had happened since then. One day, she'd see God's plan in it all.

"Well at least the smoke removal service worked wonders." Mark set a box marked DISHES on the kitchen counter. "Most of our stuff survived. And for the first time since you moved out of Mom and Dad's, you'll have a yard to call your own."

Small comfort.

"And most of your garden came with you." Rachel joined an obvious effort to point out the positives.

"Surprise." Mark set a pet carrier on the floor and opened the door.

Tripod clambered out, big-eyed, taking in the new surroundings.

"Hey, baby." Tripod curled himself around Adrea's ankles. She picked up the less-than-whole feline and he rubbed against her, motor running. "Oh, Mark, thank you."

"Since the floors are tile, the landlord said we can have pets. I might even build a fence in the back."

The location of the rental house was farther from Rose Bud and Grayson's stomping grounds. She wouldn't have to worry about seeing him every time she turned around when he came back.

"This is a good move. I'll be fine here."

❧

Adrea stared out the dining room window. The early November wind howled with brown, falling refuse to be raked, bagged, and burned.

Something brushed against her hand. Her breath caught and she whirled around, sloshing coffee.

"Whoa." Mark righted her cup. "How many have you had?"

"Three. It's not helping. Is he back?"

"Yes. And if it's any consolation, he doesn't look happy, either." Mark flashed an impish grin.

"It's not. You didn't hit him again, did you?"

"On the contrary, I pretended to be absolutely overjoyed to see him." He motioned toward his tie.

"Good boy." She made the loops and pulled the burgundy and gray striped silk into a neat knot. "How's Dayne?"

"He seemed a little sad, too. I think he misses you. He asked about you a dozen times."

"I miss him, too."

"It's a shame his father is such a jerk."

"Mark!"

"Well, it is." He kissed her cheek. "Ready?"

"You really should go to Palisade."

"I've got the day off and I choose to go with my family for a change."

She hugged him, grateful for his support.

Ten minutes later, they arrived at Mountain Grove for the first time in eight months. As she stepped inside, it felt like old-home week. Their parents, Rachel, Curt, and Haylee welcomed them, as did all their friends. They met several new people who had begun attending during their absence.

Adrea missed the harp, but it didn't matter at all that Palisade was a prettier church. No one asked why she was back. As usual, Mom had smoothed things for her.

After class, small arms snaked around her waist. Expecting one of the children she used to teach, Adrea was shocked to see Dayne.

"Dayne! Oh, how I've missed you." She knelt to his level and returned the exuberant hug. "What are you doing here?"

"I wanted to see you, so Grace said we could visit your church. I miss you. And Haylee."

"We miss you, too." Tears blurred her vision. She blinked them away. "She's around here somewhere."

"Why did you leave our church? Didn't you like teaching me?"

"I loved being your teacher, Dayne." She stood and tousled his hair. "Really. But Mrs. Roberts is well now."

"I'm glad she's all better since her heart attacked her. I like her and all." Dayne shrugged. "But I liked when you was my teacher, too. Why aren't you and Daddy friends no more? Why don't you come to our house no more, and how come me and Haylee don't get to spend the night with you and Mark no more?"

"Oh, sweetie, it's complicated."

Grace and Mark joined the reunion, rescuing Adrea from Dayne's probing questions.

Haylee rushed over. "Can I take Dayne out to the swing set?"

"For just a few minutes, but stay away from the parking lot." Adrea brushed the little girl's bangs from her eyes. "It's almost time for service to start, and it's too cold to be out for long."

"We wanted to ask you something." Grace's voice echoed her apprehension.

"What?"

"We'll understand if you say no." Mark rubbed his chin.

"What?" Adrea repeated.

"Will you be my maid of honor?"

"Oh, Grace." Adrea hugged her soon-to-be sister-in-law. "Why would you think I might say no?"

"Because I've asked Grayson to be my best man." Mark chewed the inside of his jaw.

Her stomach twisted. "Well, it's good that the two of you are getting along so well."

"I'm trying to mend fences." Mark hung his head. "For Grace's sake."

"I'm proud of you." She patted his shoulder, then turned to the radiant woman beside him. "Grace, it will be my privilege to serve as your maid of honor."

"Are you sure? I really want you to, but the last thing we want is for you to feel uncomfortable."

"All I'll feel is happiness for you two." She stepped between them and put her arms around both their shoulders. "Did Mark tell you that I want to do the flowers free? Whatever you want, it's my wedding gift to you."

"That is so sweet of you, but it's too much."

"It's not too much. It'll be my pleasure."

"Well, when you get married, you've got a free caterer, at your service." Grace realized her blunder, with a rare blush.

An awkward silence ensued. The choir music began.

"Excuse me," Adrea said. "I better get up there. The song service is about to begin."

"I'll get the kids." Grace hurried toward the door.

After the choir finished, she sat with her parents, with

Dayne beside her. She enjoyed the service, but had a difficult time concentrating on Curt's sermon. Instead, her thoughts kept straying to Grayson.

After church, Mark hitched a ride with Grace. They invited Adrea to lunch, but she begged off.

On the way home, she noticed movement along the side of the highway. Two dogs; a starved German shepherd and a skinny bloodhound. She pulled to the shoulder. The larger dog backed away, shivering with fear and cold. It walked with a limp and its right hind leg had dried blood on it. The hound came right to her, limping, its pads raw. Most of its left ear was missing. With very little coaxing, it jumped into the backseat.

"Let's see, you're a hunting dog. We'll call you Coon." The dog nuzzled his velvety muzzle in her hand, looking for anything edible. "We'll go to the store and get you some food, as soon as I get your friend in the car."

The shepherd was a different story. She finally gave up and went to the store. Thirty minutes later, with a raw hamburger incentive, Mouse got into her car.

❧

The Thursday after his return, Adrea stopped by Helen's on her way home from work. Expecting the subject of Grayson to surface, her stomach churned.

"Adrea, what perfect timing." Helen swung the door open wide, leaning on her cane. "I just got these out of the oven."

Adrea sniffed the air. Fruit and cake. Blueberry muffins.

Helen slathered butter on two, set them on saucers with delicate blue flowers around the rim, and handed one to Adrea.

"Eat up, while it's still warm." Helen took a bite.

Adrea sank her teeth into the moist, savory confection. "You'll ruin my supper."

Helen shot her a conspiratorial grin. "We're adults, we can have our dessert first. Sit down, dear." Helen fixed her a cup of coffee. "I missed you at church yesterday."

Adrea swallowed hard. "Mark doesn't need me there anymore. I'm going back to Mountain Grove."

"Now, you know I'm not nosy, and I certainly don't mean to drag up a painful subject." She held up her hand when Adrea started to speak. "Let me say my piece. I'm just concerned. I know you and Pastor Grayson aren't seeing one another anymore. And I feel so bad."

"Why?" Adrea sipped her coffee.

"Wade has caused so much heartache for you both." The aged blue eyes grew watery. "I felt so much better about things, since the two of you were moving on. Together."

"None of it's your fault."

"I can't help taking part of the responsibility."

"Did you raise Wade to believe it was okay to drink?"

"Of course not."

"Then you can't blame yourself, Helen." Adrea patted her hand. "He made his own choices."

"Did you know Grayson goes with me to see him? While he was gone, Grace went."

He'd never mentioned it, not even when they'd been almost engaged. "I can go with you anytime."

A knock sounded at the door.

"You're expecting someone? I could have come another day."

"Stop worrying yourself. I'm not expecting anyone." Helen made moves to get up. Though her hip had healed completely, she still moved more stiffly and slowly than before, relying on her cane for support.

"Let me get it." Adrea peeked out the high window in the heavy pine door and immediately wished she could melt into the floor. All she could see was his hair and forehead, but she'd know him anywhere.

Adrea swung the door open and greeted him with a forced smile. "Hello, Grayson."

"Adrea." His voice and raised brows reflected his surprise.

"She still visits me a few times every week. Isn't she a doll?" Helen asked. "Some man will be lucky to get her."

Adrea grasped for a subject change. "How's Dayne?"

"Okay. He enjoyed the trip."

Grayson looked tired and worn, but still handsome.

"Where did you go? Dayne didn't say."

"The Grand Canyon. I always promised we'd go there, but Sara never made it. I decided to make sure Dayne and I did."

The try at casual conversation felt strained. They both fell silent for a moment.

"Well, I really need to get home," Adrea said.

"Please don't leave on my account."

"Don't go just yet, Adrea." Helen patted the sofa to her left. "Sit with me. I'm leaving for Thanksgiving at June's tomorrow and I'll be gone a whole week."

Obediently, Adrea sat.

"I was about to tell you a story. You'll like this one, too, Pastor Grayson." Helen patted the sofa to her right.

"I do love your stories." He sat on the other side of the older woman.

"Did I ever tell you about my older sister, Ruthie?"

"No."

"She passed a few years ago, didn't she?" Adrea concentrated on breathing evenly.

"She's with the Lord now. But when she was young, she met this man, fell for Herb hard, and he worshipped the ground she walked on. Both of them were strong in the Lord, put Him first in everything. They were perfect for each other. Just as the whole town started buzzing about wedding bells, *poof*, it was over."

"What happened?" The story drew Adrea, despite the handsome man across from her.

"Don't know. Ruthie never would talk about it, but I know, until her dying day, she loved Herb. No one could bring up his name without her bursting into tears." Helen paused to wipe away one of her own. "Long about five years after the breakup, she married. She and Ernest raised three kids. Now, he loved her dearly and she loved him, in her way. But, not like Herb."

Grayson cleared his throat.

"Poor Herb never married, pined for Ruthie the rest of his life. Ruthie went on, but she never was as happy and Ernest knew she didn't love him as she should have. Now, why would people want to do that?" Helen held both hands out, palms up. "God gives them someone to love and cherish and they snub their noses at His gift."

Adrea took Helen's hand. "I enjoyed visiting with you, as usual, but I really do need to go. I have to get dinner on, though I'm not hungry, thanks to those scrumptious muffins."

"I put a couple aside for Mark." Helen gestured to the table. "There, wrapped in foil."

"He'll love you for it." Adrea retrieved the goodies.

Grayson walked her to the door as she forced her pace to slow.

"It's always nice to see you. You look well."

"You, too."

Their eyes met and held.

With a wave at Helen, Adrea fled.

❧

Adrea checked the computer. November 18th, Grayson and Sara's anniversary. The order was still there. Would Grayson keep his standing order at the shop or take his business elsewhere?

Rachel stepped through the door from the showroom holding a long white box tied with yellow ribbon. "Do you want this?"

"Yes."

Rachel patted her arm and went to the office.

Adrea opened the box. A single yellow rose. *He must simply want to torture me.* She forced herself to read the card.

Dear Adrea,

I hope you are doing well. After wrestling with myself about whether to find a new florist, I concluded that you are the best. You truly love Sara. No other florist would do her justice. I won't disturb you when I pick up the arrangement. However, if you feel led to discontinue your services, I'll understand completely. I'm sorry for everything.

Sincerely,
Grayson

"Rachel," Adrea called.

Her sister stepped out of the office. "You rang?"

"Will you call Grayson and tell him that his business is always welcome here?"

"Are you sure? It would be much easier on you if he went elsewhere."

"Yes, it would be, but it wouldn't be right."

With an understanding nod, Rachel went back to the office to make the call.

Adrea resolutely began the arrangement of white roses for Sara. More tears spilled as she cried harder over the flowers than ever before. Only two months before, she'd joined Grayson at the cemetery for Dayne's birthday.

Rachel returned, but wisely said nothing when she saw the tears. She simply took the array to the showroom.

Adrea didn't relax until she heard that Grayson and Dayne had come and gone.

≈

The week after Thanksgiving, Adrea arranged flowers for two funerals. As the back door opened behind her, she assumed it was Rachel, back from a delivery and ready for the next.

"I'm finishing the last spray. Just give me a minute."

"Hello, Adrea."

For a few seconds, she couldn't bring herself to turn toward the voice. Finally, after what seemed like an eternity, she turned to see Grayson, just as handsome as ever.

"Hello." She controlled the quiver in her voice.

"It's good to see you. You look great."

"You, too." A few more lines around his eyes.

"Dayne misses you."

"I miss him, too. It was wonderful to see him at church."

"He said you sang in the choir. Why didn't you join the choir at Palisade?"

"Your church had a large choir already, so I wasn't needed. Mountain Grove wouldn't let me off the hook." It seemed odd speaking of trivial things while her heart hammered.

"You shouldn't keep your talents under wraps." He stuffed

his hands into his jean pockets. "Look, I promised not to bother you, but I'm here on Dayne's behalf. Do you think you could occasionally find time for him?"

"What do you mean?" Adrea concentrated on the carnations.

"He misses you. He hasn't stopped asking to see you. I probably would have given in sooner, but the holidays kept him somewhat occupied." Grayson shifted his weight from one foot to the other. "The other day, he said all he wanted for Christmas is to see you."

Adrea's heart clenched. "How sweet."

"You were good for him, and he shouldn't have to lose you simply because we're no longer seeing one another."

"I'd love to see him." She nodded. "How about tomorrow night and then once a week? There's usually nothing happening on Thursday nights unless of course a holiday falls on it, but we can work around that."

"That sounds good. Dayne will be excited. Should I drop him at your place?"

"I can pick him up." *Please don't show up on my porch.* "At least, let me retrieve him."

"That's okay. We might even go to Searcy anyway, so I can take the Rose Bud route. I'll come to get him at six o'clock and have him back by nine o'clock. That's not too late for a school night, is it?"

"Sounds good. Maybe this will help. Dayne had a hard time with the abrupt ending of our relationship."

He's not the only one. "I hope seeing me won't confuse him." Adrea kept a smile plastered on her face.

"We'll have a long talk tonight and make sure he understands things. It's my fault that he had a rough time and I really appreciate this, Adrea. It will help him adjust."

"Maybe Haylee can come sometimes, too, just like old times." *Almost.*

"That would be great. Well, it was good seeing you. Take care."

"You, too." She smiled harder.

Grayson left.

A full minute passed before Adrea could relax the muscles in her face. The spray she'd been working on was a complete disaster. She pulled it apart to start over.

❧

As soon as Adrea stopped her car in the drive, Dayne rushed to jump in the back. She waved to Grace, who stood on the white-columned porch.

"I wish things were like before," Dayne whined. "I wish we could stay here with Daddy."

"We'll have fun."

"Everything's just different. I missed you on Thanksgiving. I begged Daddy to let me see you at the shop when we picked up Mommy's flowers last time, but he said you were too busy."

Her heart clenched. "You may tell your father that I'm never too busy to see you."

"I wanted you to come to the cemetery. Maybe you can come with us for Valentine's Day."

"Don't count on it, sweetie." Adrea patted his hand as she turned onto the highway. "At least we're getting to see each other now, even though things are different. I've looked forward to tonight all day long."

"Me, too."

The boy's mannerisms so reflected Grayson's that spending time with him painfully reminded her of spending time with his father. "How about Dexter's?"

"Dexter's, Dexter's, Dexter's."

She laughed. "I'll take that as a yes."

At the restaurant, numerous birthday celebrations caused the usual ruckus.

"Dayne," a familiar voice called.

Adrea turned to see Edward Owens scoop up his grandson. "Hello, Adrea. It's nice to see you."

"Yes. You, too." Adrea shook the hand he offered.

"Run and say hi to Grandma. We're just about to leave." Edward motioned to a long table to their left.

Joyce's gaze was riveted to Adrea.

"It's not what you think." She swallowed hard. "Grayson and I are no longer seeing one another."

"I was sorry to hear that. He and Dayne miss you."

"Dayne and I have a date once a week."

"We're here for our friend's grandson. We actually called to see if Dayne wanted to come, but Grayson said he already had plans. I'm glad it was with you. You're good for him and for Grayson, too."

Adrea didn't know what to say.

"Looks like the party's breaking up. I'll send Dayne back in your direction."

"Thank you."

☙

The weeks before Christmas passed in a flurry of activity, poinsettia plants, and church services.

The Welches enjoyed their traditional Christmas celebration with thoughtful gifts and scripture readings. Adrea steeped herself in the whole meaning of Jesus's birth.

The next week brought Mark and Grace's wedding preparations. Adrea spent her time obtaining even more poinsettias of every color from the wholesaler.

Their parents arrived to ride with Adrea and Mark to the rehearsal.

"I just hate to think of you living here." While Adrea primped, Mom perched on the bed, with Tripod curled in her lap, purring a steady hum. "Especially with Mark moving out."

"I'm fine."

"So, nothing's different between you and Grayson?"

"It's old news, Mom. It's over between us."

"This is your mother. I can see the hurt written all over your face. I know how much you loved him."

"I can't talk about it." Adrea's stomach knotted. "I've got to get through this wedding. For Mark's and Grace's sake, I can't think about Grayson."

"Very well, then. Oh, I meant to tell you, the florist shop in Heber Springs is up for sale."

"It is?"

"Mrs. Johnson is retiring. Speaking of retiring." Mom paused to massage her wrist. "My supervisor talked me into transferring instead, to the Rose Bud office. I start training my replacement soon. A real sweet gal, Laren Kroft."

"Kroft. I wonder if she's related to Sylvie?" Adrea checked her watch. "We need to go."

Ten minutes later, they arrived at the church. The rehearsal wore on Adrea as she walked the aisle to stand across from Grayson a dozen times.

Sara's parents arrived to sing a duet for the wedding. Though Edward greeted Adrea warmly, Joyce avoided her. Adrea couldn't blame her. They'd painfully learned Grayson was dating and given their approval, only to watch the relationship falter.

She diligently managed to avoid Grayson's parents.

By the time the rehearsal was over, she was as jittery as a helium balloon with its string caught in a box fan.

The bridal party settled in the large fellowship hall for dinner. Seated at one end of the long table with Grayson far on the other, Adrea made a mental note to thank the bride and groom for their arrangements. Even so, she was glad when the evening ended.

❧

On New Year's Eve, Adrea grabbed her scarlet satin dress, said a prayer for strength, and headed to Palisade.

She spent an hour on decorations. Placing and re-placing each spray, candelabra, and archway until Grace was completely satisfied. After the bride went to prepare for her wedding, Adrea ducked into the ladies' room and changed into her dress. Stepping back into the hall, she saw Emma Sterling headed in her direction.

Kindness radiated from Grayson's mother. Emma would never broach the subject of the broken relationship. Guilt needled Adrea for avoiding Emma at the rehearsal.

Emma hugged her. "It's so good to see you again. You look lovely in that color. It brings out the auburn highlights in your hair."

"Thank you. I thought Rachel got all those." She ran her hand over her hair. "I was so busy last night, I didn't even get to speak with you."

"Graham and I got to sit with your parents at the dinner. They're always so delightful."

"I'm glad. I've enjoyed doing this wedding more than any other." *Except for rubbing elbows with your son.*

"And you did a fabulous job, as usual. Well, I'm off to see the bride." Emma waved.

"That's where I'm headed. See you in a few minutes."

Vibrant red, faded salmon, lush burgundy, and creamy white poinsettias filled the church. Gold ribbons gathered small bouquets festooning the first several pews. Adrea inspected the decor one last time before going to find Grace. On her way, she ran into Mark and Grayson.

Trying to ignore her brother's attractive companion, wearing a chocolate tuxedo, she surveyed Mark's white one. She straightened his tie and hugged him. "You look so handsome. I'm so happy for you and Grace."

"You're quite lovely yourself. Grace and I really want you to consider moving in with us."

"I'm fine and I doubt you'll miss Mouse. He certainly won't miss you."

"Who's Mouse?" Grayson asked.

"A German shepherd. Our new landlord allows pets, so Adrea's been collecting strays. His leg was full of rat shot, and he's terrified of men. He hides under her bed most of the time."

"Doesn't sound like much of a watchdog." Grayson cleared his throat. "I can check on Adrea occasionally, until you get back from your honeymoon."

"That won't be necessary." She answered too quickly. "Coon is a good watchdog."

"Until he bellows." Mark curled his lip, Elvis style. "Anyone with ears can tell he ain't nothin' but a hound dog."

She wanted to smile at her brother's antics, knowing he was trying to help her relax, but the muscles around her mouth wouldn't comply. "I better go help the bride."

"Tell her I love her." Mark blushed.

"My tie could use your expertise." Grayson stepped close to her. "And my boutonniere, too."

Giggles surrounded them and she turned to see several teenage girls from the youth group staring. One girl pointed up.

Adrea looked up to see mistletoe directly above. Her face warmed.

eleven

Adrea bolted.

In a small classroom, Grace glowed with happiness and didn't seem nervous at all. Emma buzzed around her daughter, fluffing her train and perfecting the curls Grace rarely wore.

"Mark said he loves you." Adrea blew her a kiss. "He even blushed."

The bride's smile brightened even more. "He's so cute when he blushes."

Rachel squeezed Adrea's hand and whispered, "You okay?"

"I'm fine."

The women trickled out of the classroom as the time for the ceremony neared.

As the music swelled, Rachel walked the aisle, with Curt and Mark waiting at the front. Adrea's turn came and she concentrated on keeping her eyes off the other man waiting there with her brother. Grayson stood at the pulpit to perform the ceremony until their father handed Grace over to Mark. Then the Sterling patriarch, Graham, took over as Grayson slipped back into his role as best man.

The two became one in the sight of God and many witnesses. The well-wishers congratulated, cameras flashed, the servers cut the cake, and all too soon it was time for the bride and groom to leave for their honeymoon.

Mark hugged her. "Yo, Adrea, I wish you'd stay with Mom and Dad."

"I'm fine. Really." Anything but fine; she hadn't really thought about saying good-bye to Mark. It was just like when he'd left for seminary only this time he wasn't coming back, to their rental house, anyway. She held her tears until the happy couple disappeared.

Before helping with the cleanup, she grabbed her coat and went out in the courtyard to gather her composure.

She missed Mark, and coupled with the many encounters with Grayson over the last month, it was all too much.

Frigid air chilled her, but she didn't care. She hugged herself.

❧

Grayson stared down the highway, long after he could no longer hear the clunking trail of cans tied to Mark's car.

The tux did little to keep him warm, but at the moment he couldn't face anyone. He'd lost her. Adrea had avoided him all evening and why shouldn't she?

"Gray." His mother touched his shoulder. "You'll freeze to death out here."

He turned to face her. "I'm okay."

She cupped his cheek in her hand. "Go home, son. Dayne is having a great time helping with the cleanup. He can spend the night with us."

"I should stay to help."

"We've got plenty of help. Go." She patted his cheek. "I think you've had enough for one day."

With a nod, he kissed her forehead. He'd parked on the other side of the church and decided to walk around.

Someone stood in the lit courtyard. Someone beautiful wearing a red dress.

"Adrea?"

She jumped and with jerky movements, wiped away tears.

He wished the tears were for him, but he knew better.

"You'll miss Mark. I'll miss Grace. I don't know what Dayne and I will do without her."

She took a soggy breath. "Grace still plans to babysit Dayne after school and during the summer."

"She offered, but I want her to have plenty of time for her new husband as well as her business. Mom and Joyce have agreed to fill in."

"I better go help with the cleanup efforts."

"I wanted to speak with you." He stepped closer.

She backed away. "About?" Her breath puffed a cloud between them.

"Us."

"There is no us." One delicate hand clutched the patio railing so hard her knuckles turned white.

"I've been thinking about you a lot. I miss you."

"Just leave it alone, Grayson." Adrea made a mad dash back inside.

❧

Sheets of rain assaulted Adrea's windshield wipers, rendering them useless. Traffic putted along blindly. When she could no longer see the yellow line, she pulled over to wait out the onslaught.

For two weeks, she'd avoided Rose Bud and Grayson. But her luck couldn't hold forever. She had to get out of this town.

The escape route continued to percolate in her tired brain. But, she'd been the one to talk her sister into their partnership. She couldn't run out on Rachel.

After a few minutes, the deluge ebbed and she edged into the flow again. Just as she parked outside the shop, the sky opened up once more.

She dashed for the door. A gust of wind nearly sucked the ineffective umbrella from her hand, and by the time she made it inside, she was soaked through. Pushing damp bangs from her eyes, she checked the first order of the day and read Rachel's note. All the flowers for both weddings were complete, except for the bridal bouquets. *Hope it stops raining.*

As soon as Rachel entered from the showroom, Adrea made her plea.

"How would you feel about buying the florist shop in Heber Springs?"

"It's for sale?"

"Mrs. Johnson is retiring." Adrea clustered pink roses together in the center of a rounded bouquet. "I don't think I can take another Valentine's Day. Not here."

"Who would run it?"

The hum of the busy showroom grew louder as the connecting door opened, then faded away as it shut.

"I'd move there."

"You're moving?"

She turned at the sound of his voice and found the reason for all her heartache standing behind her.

"Ahem." Rachel cleared her throat. "I'll just be out front."

Adrea turned away from him and concentrated on the roses. "We're thinking about buying the shop in Heber Springs. It's a good business move and someone has to run it."

"What about your family?"

"I'll visit often."

"What about Dayne?"

"I'll still be here for a while, and he'll see me when I'm in town."

"What about me?"

"It doesn't concern you."

"I still love you, Adrea."

The breath whooshed out of her lungs.

"Do you still love me?"

She worked on the roses more frantically, entwining much more baby's breath than necessary.

Grayson moved to stand beside her and placed his fingers under her chin, forcing her to meet his eyes.

Her tears welled.

"Yes, but what good does that do us? You're afraid to love me."

"Grace's wedding made everything clear. By breaking up with you, I lost you, which is what I tried to avoid by breaking up with you. This isn't making any sense."

Her heart did a somersault. "You're making perfect sense, for the first time in months."

"If, God forbid, anything happens to you, He'll be there to put me back together, like He did three years ago. He's shown me that I need to turn all fears over to Him and rely on Him for my happiness, instead of earthly relationships. God has given me the strength to love you. I need you, Adrea. My son needs you."

She pressed a hand to her tremulous lips. "What if something happens to shake that strength? What if you change your mind again? My heart can't take another breakup."

Grayson took her hands. "I need to tell you about the accident."

"You don't have to."

"Yes, you need to know the details. It will help you understand me. People who plan to get married need to understand one another."

Adrea's mouth went dry. She couldn't have spoken, even if her whirling brain could have formed words.

He scooted two tall stools out of the corner.

Obediently, she sat, facing him.

"As you know, Dayne and I were also in the accident. Thankfully, he was in his car seat and came out unscathed. I remained conscious the entire time rescuers worked to cut us out."

Adrea watched Grayson mentally relive the past. His pained expression put an ache in her heart.

"My legs were pinned, so I couldn't move. Dayne was screaming at the top of his lungs, but I couldn't get to him. I could touch him, but couldn't get him out of his car seat to hold him or comfort him."

Tears glistened in his eyes. "Sara looked fine but was unconscious. After a while, her breathing became more and more labored. Though she never came to, she coughed up blood a couple of times.

"She started gurgling. Her breathing grew more difficult and infrequent, until it stopped. A paramedic worked on her through the broken windshield, but it wasn't enough. She drowned in her own blood, with me sitting right next to her. Completely powerless."

Adrea stood and wrapped her arms around him. "I'm so sorry."

"When I saw your apartment building on fire, I felt that helplessness again. That night, I dreamed of the accident, the sound of Sara struggling to breathe, and Dayne crying. This time, after a while, it wasn't Sara beside me, but you. Then the car caught fire."

"Oh, Grayson."

They held each other, tears mingling, before he managed to pull himself together.

"Loving you still frightens me, but I can't live my life in fear and lose you. I'd rather love you and risk losing you. I'm tired of wasting time when we could be together."

The showroom door opened. "Oh my." Rachel gasped.

Adrea and Grayson disentangled themselves.

Rachel grinned and backed toward the showroom. "I'll just go find a plant to water."

❧

On Valentine's Day, the showroom door opened and Dayne burst through. "Pretty flowers."

"For a pretty lady."

Dayne flew into Adrea's arms as Grayson joined them. "I'm so glad you and Daddy are friends again."

"Me, too." She glanced at Grayson.

He joined the embrace, his chin resting on top of her head. "Will you come to the cemetery with us today? One last time."

Adrea frowned but didn't ask questions and grabbed her jacket. "Sure."

Fifteen minutes later, they arrived at the cemetery. Adrea's black heels sank into the red clay, but despite the chill in the air, her heart sang. The threesome held hands as Dayne carried the white roses for his mother.

She no longer felt like an interloper when it came to Sara. Instead, Adrea felt as if Sara's torch, to love and care for those she left behind, had been passed on. She willingly complied.

Dayne solemnly placed the flowers and polished the headstone while his father tidied the grave. Adrea stood off to the side with a sense of belonging.

"Son, head to the car. We'll be there in a few minutes."

"Okay." The boy hurried in that direction.

He took both of Adrea's hands. "I've wasted so much time.

I never thought I'd be happy again after Sara died, but God sent me you. And I almost blew it." He kissed her forehead. "I've asked Sara's parents to do the flowers in the future. I'll only come on Valentine's Day, and I won't bring Dayne anymore, unless he asks."

"Are you sure?"

"Dayne and I need to move forward." He tucked her hand into his elbow and turned toward the car. "With you."

His words warmed her heart. She snuggled against his side.

❧

The next day, Grayson sat at his desk at the church. Footsteps headed his way and he looked up to see Mark.

"Good, just the person I need to see." Mark closed the office door.

He didn't look happy about it.

Grayson offered his hand.

Mark ignored it.

"What's on your mind?"

"My sister."

"Isn't that a coincidence? She's on my mind, too." Grayson smiled, but it died on his lips when Mark didn't match his cheerfulness.

"Look, as long as Adrea is happy, there'll be no interference from me. But if you hurt her again, you'll have me to answer to."

"I'm well aware of that." Grayson rubbed his stomach as if it were still tender from Mark's blow. "I love your sister. I've talked with God about her and placed her in His hands. Through His strength, I can move on."

"You're sure?"

Grayson opened his mouth.

Mark raised his hand to silence him. "Let me finish. You've been through a lot and my concerns may seem callous. But, are you certain that you're ready this time?"

"I plan to propose. Our life together can't begin soon enough for me."

Mark nodded. "Adrea deserves to be happy."

"I'll do my utmost to never hurt her again."

The two men shook hands.

❧

Adrea hummed as she put together a bridal spray. Early March brought preparations for the first spring wedding of the year. The showroom door opened and she turned to find her very own prince.

"Close your eyes." He shot her a devilish grin.

"What are you up to?"

"I'm kidnapping you."

"Sounds heavenly, but I have a wedding today."

"Rachel promised to handle it."

Tears pricked her eyes.

"What?" His hand cupped her cheek.

"I'm not used to having a man care about my schedule or my business."

"Get used to it." He kissed the tip of her nose. "Everything's taken care of. Now close your eyes."

Shivers moved over her as she obeyed. A soft linen cloth draped over her face and she could feel Grayson tying it in place, careful not to pull her hair. Spicy cologne filled her senses.

His arm came around her waist and he walked her out.

"It better not be very far. The suspense will drive me mad."

Adrea lost all sense of direction as Grayson drove. Each turn took her stomach.

"Is it much farther?"

He stopped the car. "Actually, we're here." His car door opened, then hers, and he helped her out.

"Can I see now?"

"Not yet." With his arm around her waist again, he walked her across bumpy ground. "Slight step up."

Level, a sidewalk perhaps.

"Now, three steps down."

Water. The rush of water.

"Romance Waterfalls."

"You've been here before?" He sounded disappointed.

"Eight steps down."

"I've done two weddings here, but I always love coming." She touched the blindfold. "Can't I see now? I'm missing all the landscaping."

"Not just yet. Five steps down."

She followed his instructions and the sound of rushing water grew louder, until finally, he stopped and removed the handkerchief.

They stood on the balcony overlooking the waterfall. The water crashed over jutting rocks.

"Even though I've seen it before, I've never seen it with you." She turned to scan the flower beds, kept fresh looking with silk blossoms in the winter.

"Good, I wanted this to be special." He knelt on one knee. "Will you marry me?"

"Oh, Grayson."

"Is that a yes?"

"Yes."

Grayson swept her into his arms. He had proven Rachel was right, after all. Men do indeed sweep women into their arms.

"Let's get married on Easter. We usually dismiss evening services. What better time for a wedding?"

Joy welled in her soul. "Can we pull a wedding together that fast?"

"We'll put an army on it, my mom, yours, Grace, Rachel, Helen."

She pulled away to look into his eyes. "At Palisade. A fresh start for both of us."

"We'll create good memories. Together."

❧

Adrea thought back to when Grayson announced their engagement at church this morning. Everyone applauded. After services, well-wishers surrounded Adrea. Sylvie's friends offered congratulations, but Sylvie didn't.

Despite Sylvie's disapproval, it was no longer Grayson and Sara, but Grayson and Adrea. He spoke of his first wife less as he and Adrea developed a history of their own. Their names were now synonymous to those who knew them.

The smell of charbroiled burgers beckoned her back to setting the table. She rubbed her chilled hands together. Crazy. Who else would grill outdoors in the middle of March? But Dayne loved it.

She caught Tripod. "Away from the table, or I'll lock you in the house."

"Have you settled the new shop yet?" Grayson asked.

"I promise it will all be under control before the wedding. I'll find a great manager, so I won't have to go there but maybe once a month."

"Make it happen sooner." He flipped the burgers. "I'm tired of our bicoastal relationship."

"It's only two days a week and not that far." The nagging at her conscience wouldn't let up. "Have you talked to Edward and Joyce about our wedding?"

"Yes."

"And?"

"It's hard on them, but they're happy for us."

"I think we have one more thing to take care of before we can move forward. Do you think your mom or Grace could watch Dayne after supper?"

"Tonight?" He quirked an eyebrow.

"I'd like to get it over with."

&

By the time Grayson parked in the Owens' drive, Adrea's whole body trembled.

"I can do this." He squeezed her hand.

"No, it's my place." She jumped out of the car and hurried to the door, but he halted her.

"Okay, but do what you have to do. Then go."

"I can't drop my bomb and skulk away. What will they think of me?"

He smoothed her hair. "I don't want anything said in a moment of shock that could hurt for a lifetime."

Adrea shook her head.

"Okay, I'll leave with you, take you home, then come back

to check on them." Grayson waited until she nodded, then rang the doorbell.

"Well, how nice to see you," Edward said. "Come in. I hear congratulations are in order."

She was thankful for his always gracious attitude. In contrast, Joyce looked anything but happy.

"Joyce, sorry to bother you without calling first." Grayson hugged his former mother-in-law. "Adrea and I need to clear some things up."

"Oh."

There wasn't any way to ease into it, and her heart felt as if it would surely burst from her chest. "I was engaged to Wade Fenwick."

"Oh, my." Joyce clasped her hand to her heart and reclaimed her seat on the sofa.

Adrea felt the blood drain from her face.

"Let me." Grayson tried to steer her toward the door.

"No, they should hear it from me." Adrea closed her eyes. "He'd been sober for two years when we met. Shortly before our wedding, I learned he'd been unfaithful, and I called off the engagement."

"Do we really need to do this?" Edward pulled his wife into his arms. "I'd just as soon never hear anything about that dreadful man. It's past history; what does it matter?"

"But it does matter." Adrea stared at the floor. "Our wedding day would have been February 14th, three years ago. He started drinking again because of our breakup."

Edward's face crumpled and a sob escaped Joyce.

Grayson urged Adrea toward the door.

"I'm sorry. Truly I am, but I—we—were afraid you'd hear it from someone else and be angry with us for not being honest with you."

Grayson hurried her outside.

Feeling cowardly, she wiped her eyes and looked toward the house next door. A redhead ducked behind the swaying curtains.

Adrea pulled away from Grayson and ran to his car.

On Easter evening, the twenty-six-year-old bride sat in one of Mountain Grove's classrooms. While Rachel wove baby's breath into Adrea's dark hair, Grace applied pale pink nail polish. Emma and Mom fluffed and clucked nervously as Adrea calmly sat in the midst of all the fuss.

When the door opened, all eyes turned, fearing the groom might have decided to do away with traditions. Instead, Joyce stood uncertainly in the entrance.

"Adrea, you look lovely."

"Thank you." She smiled, hoping her nervousness didn't show. "This is my mother, Samantha Welch, and my sister, Rachel. This is Joyce Owens, Sara's mother."

The women exchanged greetings.

Joyce turned her attention back to the bride. "I was hoping to speak with you."

Her stomach did a somersault. "Of course. I think they've done all they can do with me."

Rachel cleared her throat, prompting the other women to begin filing out. "We'll go see how things are coming along."

Adrea looked in the mirror and applied a little more blush. The white satin sapped her fair complexion of all color.

"I owe you an apology," Joyce said.

"You don't owe me anything."

"Yes, I do." Joyce pressed her fingertips to her temple. "I treated you badly at Dexter's and at Grace's wedding. Grayson never told us what happened, until a few days ago. I assumed that you'd broken up with him. But, even if you had, I shouldn't have ignored you."

"You gave our relationship your blessing, and then we broke up." Adrea adjusted her veil with trembling fingers. "It must have seemed like added heartache for no reason. And this new revelation certainly doesn't help matters, but I felt you had a right to know."

"And you were very brave for telling us the truth." Joyce moved to the window. "I trust God's plan and His timing completely. I won't claim to understand why bad things happen in this world."

Joyce turned to face her, as Adrea's tears spilled. "Now, don't do that. You'll muss your makeup." Joyce dabbed Adrea's cheeks with a tissue. "We don't blame you."

"But if I'd married Wade, Sara would still be alive."

"I don't think so. That goes back to God's plan and timing. I believe their lives would have collided, ending Sara's, no matter what you did."

"He'd been sober for two years, until *I* broke the engagement."

"The only thing that would have come of you marrying Wade Fenwick would have been heartache for you. Men don't usually change after marriage. He would have remained unfaithful, you'd have been miserable, and some disappointment could have set him to drinking eventually." Joyce handed her another tissue.

"Or maybe he would have celebrated at your wedding reception and you'd have been in the accident, as well. Or maybe something else would have ended Sara's life, but it would have happened. It was her time to go. God only lent my angel for a short time and then He took her home."

Adrea gulped a sob, and Joyce took her hand.

"I wanted to welcome you to our family today."

Her eyes swam with tears. "That means a lot to me. Thank you."

The two women hugged.

ঙ

After repairing her makeup, Adrea and Joyce stepped into the foyer to find Edward waiting.

"Ah, looks like things are okay." He hugged Adrea. "Wade Fenwick caused you and Grayson a lot of pain. Now, God has brought the two of you together. No more looking back, only forward."

Daddy joined them. "Ready?"

Adrea nodded and the doors opened. The church echoed with the wedding march as Daddy escorted her down the aisle. Yellow roses filled every crevice and perfumed the air. Grace and Rachel, the matron of honor, dressed in yellow satin and lace with hooped skirts, stood with Haylee, the flower girl. A veritable feast waited in the fellowship hall.

Her breath caught at the sight of Grayson standing at the altar, beaming at her. Her very own Prince Sterling, resplendent in a white tuxedo with tails.

Dayne, as ring bearer, tried not to fidget. Best man, Mark, seemed almost as happy as she felt. Jack served as Grayson's groomsman while Joyce and Edward were given a seat of honor next to his mother. Helen sat with Adrea's mom, both dabbing their eyes with tissue.

Adrea's huge satin hoop skirt whispered with each stutter-step across yellow rose petals strewn by Haylee.

Love welled in her heart until she thought she might burst. God had taken the tattered pieces of her and Grayson's hearts and mended them into one.

When Graham declared Grayson and Adrea husband and wife, the sanctuary erupted with a joyful standing ovation.

Tears laced Adrea's lashes.

"You may kiss your bride."

Prince Sterling swept his bride into his arms and did just that.

A Letter To Our Readers

Dear Reader:

In order that we might better contribute to your reading enjoyment, we would appreciate your taking a few minutes to respond to the following questions. We welcome your comments and read each form and letter we receive. When completed, please return to the following:

Fiction Editor
Heartsong Presents
PO Box 719
Uhrichsville, Ohio 44683

1. Did you enjoy reading *White Roses* by Shannon Taylor Vannatter?
   ❑ Very much! I would like to see more books by this author!
   ❑ Moderately. I would have enjoyed it more if

   _____

   _____

   _____

2. Are you a member of **Heartsong Presents**? ❑ Yes ❑ No
   If no, where did you purchase this book? _____

   _____

3. How would you rate, on a scale from 1 (poor) to 5 (superior), the cover design? _____

4. On a scale from 1 (poor) to 10 (superior), please rate the following elements.

   ____ Heroine   ____ Plot
   ____ Hero   ____ Inspirational theme
   ____ Setting   ____ Secondary characters

5. These characters were special because? _____

_____

_____

6. How has this book inspired your life? _____

_____

_____

7. What settings would you like to see covered in future
   Heartsong Presents books? _____

_____

_____

8. What are some inspirational themes you would like to see
   treated in future books? _____

_____

_____

9. Would you be interested in reading other **Heartsong
   Presents** titles? ❏ Yes ❏ No

10. Please check your age range:
    ❏ Under 18   ❏ 18-24
    ❏ 25-34   ❏ 35-45
    ❏ 46-55   ❏ Over 55

Name_____

Occupation _____

Address _____

City, State, Zip_____

E-mail _____